HER BOSS

A LESBIAN/SAPPHIC ROMANCE

GRACE PARKES

1
ALEX CHAPMAN

It took Alex a second too long to realize the thin vase of tulips on her desk was tipping to the side. She blinked in surprise, tearing her eyes away from the design proposals littering her screens to watch as the tulips nearly leapt from the vase as it tumbled down. By the time they reached the floor, the tulips were joined in a splattering mess of glass, water, and plant food.

"Ahh!" Alex grunted, pushing her drawing tablet and chair to the side as the water began to spread. She stuck the tablet pen on a shelf, only for it to roll back onto the desk.

Alex sucked in an agitated breath and shoved the pen into a pile of paperwork, deftly stepping around the puddle to move the chair opposite her. She glanced around at the shelves positioned above her desk, covered with pictures and mementos, and the cabinets resting at her other side full of endless reports, but there was nothing to clean up this mess.

"She had to send me flowers of all things," Alex sighed and grumbled as she stepped back to her side of the desk. "Thank you, Mom, for yet another mess for me to clean up."

With a grimace, Alex pressed a button on her office phone, which let out a long and low beep.

"Cleaning services!" a chipper voice piped up from the receiver.

"Trina? It's Alex, again," she sighed. "Can you send someone to clean up some broken glass and spilled water in my office? I have a visitor coming in just a few minutes."

"Right away, Ma'am! Jeff will be there shortly," Trina replied.

"Thank you, Trina. I know you're short staffed, I appreciate it." Alex smiled through the phone.

"Of course, Ms. Chapman. Hope your visit goes well!"

Alex gave Trina a quick farewell before ending the call and looking around at the spill on her floor. "At this rate, I'll need a cleaner just for *my* office," she mumbled, scooting her chair to the side and settling down once again.

Alex was nearly done with the most recent batch of designs sent for approval, and she hoped this self-imposed interruption hadn't taken her too far out of the zone. This batch was primarily logo designs for a handful of homestores, tied in with the rebranding of a technology store, and a new Thai restaurant opening locally. Alex hummed to herself as she studied the images, referencing each company as she went about making a few small changes and tweaks.

As CEO, the Board Members of Chapman Signature Studios urged against Alex being directly involved with the work, but she didn't build up her own company just to lose the rights to lead the designs herself! There were some artists and designers in the firm that she trusted to put out good work, and she let them do so, but for the bigger clients, Alex liked to take on a few projects herself, or at the very least provide edits and approval for the final designs. It was the part she enjoyed most about her job, and some days, Alex made sure she'd have time to put her talents to good use.

After checking off a few designs on her list, there was a quick knock at her door before she had the chance to finish up the rest of her editing list.

"Come in," she called as a burly man in jeans and a button-up shirt stepped inside, giving Alex a curt nod before his eyes wandered to the spill on the floor. He had a simple name badge with the name *Jeff G* engraved onto it, and Alex remembered seeing him before. He was quiet and quick, but pleasant to talk to when he'd give you the chance.

"Thank you for being so prompt, Jeff." Alex smiled. "Let me know if you need anything from me, alright?"

Jeff smiled and offered a quiet, "Of course, Ma'am." He got to work cleaning up the mess, assuring Alex he would be more than careful picking up the glass when she expressed her worry. But he was a professional after all, and in no time, Jeff had the floors looking marvelous and dry again.

"Thank you, Jeff. Have a good day!" Alex said with a smile, turning away from her work to acknowledge him. Jeff gave her a curt nod in return, heading out to deal with a dozen other issues that were most certainly popping up around the building. Trina hadn't expressed the lack of staff in words, but she always seemed so frazzled that Alex wondered if they had the budget to hire a few more workers.

Just as Alex sent off the last of her logo edits, a knock at her door left her blinking at the screen in surprise.

"That's right..." she mumbled under her breath, "Sarah's visiting."

Alex quickly got the door, where one of her assistants was waiting with a beaming smile. Right next to her was a woman with short, dark, curly hair twisted up in a hair clip at the back of her head, who was notably using crutches. Alex's eyes fell to the large cast wrapped around her right foot, brow furrowing as she met the woman's gaze.

She gave Alex a smile and a bit of a shrug, but Alex spoke before she had the chance to get a word out.

"Sarah! What the hell happened?" Alex stepped forward with growing concern, holding the door open and offering her friend a hand as she stepped inside.

Sarah rolled her eyes, "It's alright, Alex. I figured it was time to visit you again, and breaking my foot was a good excuse to have the time to do so." She knocked her elbow into Alex's arm as she passed with a silly little grin, carefully making her way to the seat across Alex's desk.

Alex dismissed her assistant and let the door shut behind her. She again offered Sarah a hand as she got settled, but she wouldn't accept it. Instead, Alex quickly grabbed her office chair and wheeled it around to face Sarah. She didn't want to enhance the unnecessary distance of a desk between them when she was meeting her dearest friend.

"Now can you tell me what happened? You're not one to trip and cause an accident like this."

Sarah grimaced, stretching out in her seat while her eyes wandered about the room. "Yeah..." She began, carefully meeting Alex's gaze. "It's nothing crazy. It sort of happens from time to time when you work in construction."

Alex leaned forward in her seat. "But you're usually so careful. You've been working with this company for years, did something happen?"

"Oh, no. The company's great." Sarah shook her head. "Just took one slip up from me is all. I slipped on some scaffolding. It wasn't too high, but I landed on my foot wrong and ended up in this." She pointed to her cast with a sigh.

"Shit, that sounds awful. I'm sorry to hear that, it must be a pain in the ass."

Sarah smiled as she continued, "I appreciate it, but there's not much to change about it now. They said I could go back to work if it was healed up enough after my allotted leave, but that time came and went and...now I'm without a job."

Alex's eyes went wide. "They fired you? For that?"

Sarah grimaced again. "Well, it's a bit more complicated than that. But that's the short version, I guess."

It took a moment or two for Alex to really take in the information, but her face was growing softer and softer as the gravity of the situation hit her. "Gosh, I know this is right after your mom started getting worse. Do you need anything?"

Sarah sighed, averting her eyes. "That's the thing... I know it's been a while since I visited, we both tend to get lost in our jobs. But I *did* have a favor to ask of you..." Sarah's gaze lifted to meet Alex with a soft grimace.

Alex nodded, leaning back in her chair and loosely folding her arms. Then, after a moment of silence, she scoffed and rolled her eyes. "You make this sound like I need to give you my firstborn child or something. Of course I can do you a favor."

Sarah's face softened and she took a deep breath. "Well, I'd never intrude on you or your work unless I really had to, but...with me being out of a job, things are kind of rough right now."

Alex nodded, growing more concerned.

"I'm not asking you for money!" Sarah clarified. "You know I wouldn't accept it even if you offered. But since I can't work, Isla's been looking for a job."

"Your younger sister?" Alex asked. "I thought she wanted to be a dancer."

With a sigh, Sarah's grimace returned. "That was years ago. She's worked a number of odd jobs since, but she got laid off last year and hasn't been able to find a job since. She's super efficient and good as most things."

Alex pursed her lips, awaiting the inevitable. She did have to admit, this was all very unlike Sarah. One of the reasons they'd been so drawn to each other as friends was because of how they both loved to work hard. In college, they both had dreams of building up their careers and making their place in the world. Alex had had her own struggles, of course, but Sarah always seemed to get the short end of the stick.

"She wasn't fired for being a bad worker or anything! They just didn't have funding to support the cleaning staff at her last job. And, she doesn't need some fancy desk job or anything now," Sarah mumbled as she dragged a hand down her face with another sigh. She met Alex's eye with a gaze full of quiet desperation. "Just something to help us get by until I recover and find a new job. Please, if you have anything at all in your company, she'll do it. She's a hard worker and won't complain, I promise."

Alex thought for a moment, but the trained words were already slowly escaping her lips, "I'm afraid we don't have any openings..." Alex's expression changed to a contemplative frown, letting the idea linger in her mind for a few moments longer.

Sarah bit her lip, clearly on the edge of getting emotional.

"But..." Alex began, a spike of panic in her chest as she scrambled for the right words. Sarah was not one to cry easily, and despite her reservations at opening a new position on a whim, she couldn't bear to see her friend cry. "But we have been short on cleaning staff lately."

Sarah sat up straight, knocking one of her crutches to the floor.

"Oh! I've got it." Alex bent down to pass the crutch back to Sarah, who took it with a grateful smile. She was still on the verge of tears.

"Really? I promise I wouldn't ask if I had any other option right now. You know my mom's sick and it's only getting worse—"

"Shh," Alex smiled, leaning forward and reaching out to squeeze Sarah's hand. "It's okay. I know you. I'll talk with our head custodian, Trina, and see if we can make arrangements. I'm sure she'd be happy to have an extra set of hands. As long as Isla doesn't mind cleaning!"

Sarah nodded along, squeezing Alex's hand in return and letting out a huge sigh of relief. "That'd be wonderful. As soon as I'm well enough, I'll find a job myself and Isla can look elsewhere if you can't keep her."

Alex shook her head. "It's no trouble, we'll make things work, as long as you need."

With a nod, Sarah beckoned Alex closer, "Oh, come here already."

Alex smiled and rolled her eyes, sitting up from her chair to pull Sarah into a quick embrace. "I have your back, Sarah. We can set up a time that I can show her around in person and get her started. It'll be nice to see Isla again, it's been a while."

"Yeah, it has, hasn't it." Sarah sniffled, pulling back a touch. "I know she's admired you from a distance for a while now, so being able to work with you would be like a dream to her."

"Oh, really?" Alex laughed. "What about me is worthy of admiration?"

Sarah scoffed and gestured to the room. "This? Your own company, own office, following your dreams. I know she'll just be cleaning here but I do hope seeing what you've done helps her to pursue her dreams again one day, when things are a bit better for us."

Alex nodded. "Well, I guess I'll continue doing what I do then."

"Just...treat her well, okay?" Sarah asked quietly.

"Of course, Sarah," Alex said, leaning back in to hold her friend just a bit tighter.

2

ISLA HART

Isla had worked for dozens of companies, but never one that *looked* the way you'd think a company should look like. Never the type of building that towered above you, where workers were dressed nicely without the stench of sweat or fried food wafting from their uniform. Where there was space and respect and time to accomplish all your tasks.

Aside from the fast food and cleaning jobs she'd worked, Isla had a couple of lucky breaks as a secretary and one job as a dance instructor when she had just graduated high school, but that was ages ago, and the studio was torn down two months after she'd started working there. Nearly fifteen years later, and Isla was still trying to get by.

Early that morning, Sarah had not only given her directions to the building, but thankfully directions for inside the building as well. Isla desperately hoped the layout would be easy to pick up. She'd never worked somewhere so big or so daunting, so her number one fear—among many —was of getting lost along with making a total fool of herself, especially in front of her new boss and big sister's best friend, Alex.

The front doors were pristine glass sliding doors, and she couldn't imagine how much work it took to keep them so clear and clean from smudges. From Sarah's directions, it looked like her new boss had an office a few floors up on the right side of the building, but Sarah had mentioned that Alex might come meet her personally for a tour if she had the time.

Upon stepping inside, Isla noticed only a handful of people milling about. The spaces were open and modernized, with a few art pieces littering the walls and corners of the room as the only splashes of color in the area.

No one around her looked to be Alex, at least from what Isla remembered. The two of them had met on occasion when Sarah and Alex first became close in college—but Isla was just a child then—and later on when Alex would visit the house, but it'd been years since she last saw her. For a few years, Isla had even had a crush on Alex. She was tall, strong, gorgeous beyond belief, and exuded a sort of dominant confidence that made Isla weak in the knees. But it'd been so long since then that Isla doubted the feelings would return and was even more doubtful that the crush was ever reciprocal. A part of Isla even wondered if she'd even still recognize her.

With a glance to the side, Isla noticed the secretary watching her, so with a blush in her cheeks, Isla stepped over to the front desk with a shy smile.

"Hi," she gave the secretary a small wave, "I'm here to meet with Al—um." She paused. "I'm here to meet with Ms. Chapman. Is she available?" Isla asked hopefully.

The secretary smiled warmly back at her, but her words didn't feel quite so warm. "I'm afraid Ms. Chapman is busy right now. If you'd like, I can set you up with an appointment with her?"

Isla's heart dropped, but she nodded, opening

her mouth to respond as a firm hand fell on her shoulder from behind.

"Isla, is that you?"

Isla's heart jumped back up in her stomach at the shock. As she turned to face the stranger, she found herself face to face with a woman with cool eyes, sharp cheekbones, and a frosty smile, with a platinum blonde pixie cut to match.

"Well?" the stranger asked again. "Are you my Isla? It's been a few years, but surely you remember me."

Isla swallowed her pounding heart and nodded, taking in a big breath as she put on her best smile. "Y-yes! Yes, Alex, it's me, Isla. Sorry, I didn't quite recognize you at first. It's good to see you again." Isla couldn't help but focus on the phrasing of *my Isla*. Alex had never talked like that with her. Maybe she had with Sarah, but Isla had never really noticed if so.

Alex nodded and tilted her head, almost like she was studying Isla. "Likewise." She paused for a second, her piercing eyes taking in every inch of Isla in an instant. It almost felt like she was reading her thoughts. "Shall I show you around?" Alex added.

Isla nodded, but deep down, her heart and

mind were spiraling. She'd certainly noticed how beautiful Alex was before, certainly pondered on the fantasy of dating someone like her, but Isla had *never* been so close to her before. She was striking, and her presence commanded something deeper than respect.

In addition to the change in proximity, Alex had also changed up her hair style a bit. The last time Isla saw her, it was curled and draped a little longer to the side. Now, Alex's hair was straight and brushed back and to the side. Somehow, it made the rest of her features look sharper as well. More refined.

Alex and Sarah were both a lot older than her, and had Isla been more confident in herself, she likely would have hung out with them from time to time. Sarah had certainly invited her on occasion in the last few years, but with how successful Alex had become, she'd grown more and more intimidating. Being in her presence was like that tenfold. Yet, the way Alex carried herself seemed almost casual. Casual in the way that someone acted only when they had enough confidence and charm to never worry about such things as what people were thinking of them.

"Alright then, let's get going!" Alex said as she turned about with a swagger in her step.

The secretary was seemingly at a loss for words, but one glance her way and Isla could tell she was beyond stunned that someone like Isla would know someone like *Alex*.

"Thank you," Isla whispered to the secretary, not waiting for a response as she tagged along behind Alex. She was a few inches taller than Isla, which urged her to step a bit faster to keep up.

"Your sister explained things to me already," Alex began, slowing her gait to let Isla fall in line with her. "You'll mostly be working with Trina; she's the head cleaner here, but you'll probably see a bit of me as well," Alex said with a grin and a wink, bumping shoulders with Isla in a way that made her cheeks warm.

"Oh?" Isla asked, holding onto her own wrist as they walked through the first hallway that she was already trying to commit to memory.

"Yeah, Sarah seems a bit out of sorts right now with being stuck at home. Thought I'd do what I can to make your work here as pleasant as possible so she has less to worry about," Alex said as she turned the corner, brushing a hand against Isla's back to steer her the right direction as well. "Your primary job will be to keep my office clean. Figured that might be easier since you know me, but don't worry, Trina has lots more for you to do too. I think you'll like her."

Isla nodded along, wondering if she should pull out her phone to take notes, or simply commit everything to memory.

"Here's where home base will be for you. I'll bring you back here after showing you around so you can get to know Trina." Alex waved a hand inside an open door where a woman with dirty blonde hair waved back. She had a pleasant smile, and Isla found that comforting, at least for now.

Isla had had her fair share of good bosses, bad bosses, or bosses that just didn't care, but she hoped Trina would be good. She seemed like it from first glance. Alex herself was proving to be polite and professional, if a bit intimidating still.

As they stepped into the elevator, a few others crowded in behind them. Alex took them to the side, cornering Isla against the wall and giving her a questioning look. "You alright there, sweetie?"

Isla blushed and nodded, shrinking against the wall and looking straight ahead to avoid Alex's teasing look. She'd always known Alex was into girls, of course, it was one of the many things she and Sarah had talked about over the years. But in all her years, Isla never thought that *she* might be on the receiving end of Alex's flirting nature, even if it was just in a casual or teasing way. Even while being in her thirties now, Isla was so much younger than Alex that she doubted someone like Alex would even consider her in that way. On top of their age difference, Alex owned a successful company and seemed to have it all figured out. Isla felt like she was just starting out in life for the fifth time or so, still trying to understand where it would take her.

Isla did have to admit it was a bit of a relief to escape the elevator and how close Alex had been to her. She did her best to look attentive and alert as Alex talked her through the main areas of the building, pointing out important rooms along the way.

"Oh, remind me, on our way back to Trina's office, I'll have to show you the company break room as well as the main supply room in the building. Trina might show you again, but I figure a quick overview won't hurt anyone."

Isla nodded with a shy smile. "Thank you, I appreciate it. That sounds great to me!"

Alex looked back at Isla with a much warmer smile this time, but she didn't say anything.

Instead, the CEO turned back to the door she was facing in the hallway.

Just beyond Alex, the hallway opened up into a large office space. There were dozens of tables, chairs, computers, and people filling those spaces, moving about in a quick and quiet hustle and bustle.

"That's the main office area, most of the marketing and design teams work there. You might help out once in a while, but for the most part, you'll be in here with me." Alex quickly unlocked the room, gesturing Isla inside.

As she stepped in, Isla was immediately drawn to the shelves full of pictures, artwork, and mementos by Alex's desk. She even remembered a few of them herself from when Alex and Sarah were living together and Isla paid them a visit. She turned back to Alex before she'd be caught snooping and asked with a bit more excitement in her voice, "This is your office? It's really nice in here."

Alex smiled back at Isla and stepped over to the desk, arranging a few papers and binders as she spoke. "It is. And thank you, that's nice of you to say. Did you have any questions so far?"

Isla pondered for a moment, but shook her

head, eyes still wandering about the room to take in Alex's personal effects and decoration, as well as the areas that might need a bit more attention in the realm of cleaning. "No, but thank you. I'm just happy to be here! It's really good to see you again, Alex." Isla paused. "Or, um, should I call you Ms. Chapman here?"

With a scoff, Alex shook her head. "Call me Alex, that's more than fine. It'd feel weird to have you calling me Ms. Chapman all of a sudden."

"Okay!" Isla said, grateful she wouldn't have to be too formal with someone who felt so unapproachable, yet so familiar, all at once.

"Now..." Alex began as she got the rest of her documents situated. "Feel free to take a seat. We'll go through what things will be like for your first few days here, and then I'll take you down to Trina for the rest of your training, does that sound alright?"

"Yes, thank you Alex!" Isla nodded, taking a seat and mentally preparing herself to exceed in being a good worker as best she could.

∽

Isla was relieved to find that Trina was, in fact, a good boss. After Alex had dropped her off with Trina, the woman had given her a tour of the cleaning areas, custodial closets, supplies, laundry, and more. She was surprised to see that they even had a break room just for custodians that was more than just a musty closet. Trina had given her some onboarding materials to look over while she ate lunch, which she was amazed to find out was provided by the company.

Isla happily ate her lunch as she reviewed everything for a second time. She was feeling more and more relaxed about the whole situation, and the more she thought about it, the more she was sure she'd need to thank Alex next time she saw her. Maybe she could even give her a present or do something for her beyond what she'd be doing for work from now on. It was practically a miracle that she got this job in the first place, and an even greater miracle that Isla was already happy to be here and looking forward to seeing Alex again.

A quick buzz came and went from Isla's pocket, so she pulled out her phone to find a text from Sarah.

How is it?

Isla smiled, typing out a text.

It's been so good, Sarah! I can't begin to describe…

Then retyping it.

Sarah, I already love it here! Alex has been so nice, and I'll be working with this lady Trina, who is so kind…

Then deleting it altogether in favor of hitting the call button.

"Hey, Sarah?"

"Isla! How is it?" Sarah asked excitedly. Then, her tone changed to one of concern. "You never call, are you okay?"

Isla chuckled. "Yeah, I'm fine. I just thought it'd be nice to thank you in person. Or I guess, at least over the phone."

"So, it's good enough to prompt a phone call? I'd say that's pretty impressive."

Isla could feel Sarah grinning across the line, but she rolled her eyes in response. "It's still just a cleaning job, but everyone here has been so nice. I'll be coming home soon here after I finish my onboarding packet, and then I start for real tomorrow!"

"That's so exciting! Make sure to thank Alex for me, will ya?"

"Of course I will! I'm sure you've already thanked her a dozen times though."

Sarah scoffed, "Well, yeah. She created an opening just for you, you know."

Isla blushed, leaning back in her chair. "Wow, I didn't know that...I'll definitely tell her it's been much appreciated."

"You better. Now, tell me, what else has been good today?"

"Well, they gave me lunch, I got a tour of the place, and it looks like Alex is gonna have me in her office a lot, so that should be nice."

"Oh that sounds great! But her office is pretty small, that can't be all they have for you, right?" Sarah questioned.

"Not everything," Isla agreed. "But it sounds like Alex has a few projects in mind for me to do. I do hope I'll get to see more of the building, though, it's so pretty here!"

"I bet!" Sarah said. "I haven't seen much beyond the lobby and Alex's office. Maybe you'll have to take me on a tour yourself sometime."

Isla laughed. "Yeah, I'll ask Alex about that!" Isla glanced at the clock. "But I should probably just tell you the rest at home." Isla took a quick bite of her sandwich.

"Well, you're the one who called me," Sarah teased. "Plus, I'm dying of boredom over here."

Isla hummed, thinking through her day. "Well, everyone's been really nice, Alex included."

"Mmhmm," Sarah hummed along.

"Fortunately for me, she's even more attractive than I remember," Isla whispered with a blushing grin.

"Girl, gross. You can't just say that about my best friend!" Sarah joked.

"Well, it's true, isn't it?"

"Yeah, you would know. But don't go falling for Alex like every other girl she's been with that left with a broken heart."

Isla scoffed, "I'm not gonna fall for her. I just think it's nice that I get to work around her and I guess, look at her from time to time."

Sarah sighed, "I mean, looking is fine of course, but that's where it all starts. That's not why I set you up there, you know? I just don't want you getting hurt. I know Alex better than most and she's... complicated."

"I know, I know," Isla said. "I'm just joking, even if she *is* a big flirt."

Sarah gasped, "She hasn't tried flirting with you, has she? I'll come beat her up myself if I have to. It's unwritten rules—don't mess with your best friend's younger sister."

"No, no—" Isla interrupted. "She's just flirty in general. Don't worry, she's not making any moves. She's been very nice to me. Very respectful and polite"

Sarah paused for a second, then replied, "Alright, if you say so. I trust you both. I'm glad it's working out so far. I guess I'll let you go now, get home safe!"

"Of course! I'll see you and Mom later!"

Isla hung up the phone, reaching up to feel her rosy cheeks. She thought back to the time she'd had a real crush on Alex, but that time was long past. She definitely didn't have an issue with the flirting, though. But Isla knew she wore her heart on her sleeve. Somebody like Alex could be a dangerous temptation for sweet younger women like her.

"But..." Isla whispered to herself, "She said I could still look, right?" Isla smiled, quickly finishing off her lunch and hoping she'd get another glance of the beautiful yet unattainable Alex Chapman before going home for the day.

After finishing with her lunch, Isla returned to Trina with the completed packet. "Here you are! Is there anything else you need from me?"

Trina smiled, skimming through the paperwork. "Nope! This looks to be all in order. Thank you so much! Do you have any more questions before you head out?"

Isla scrunched up her face in thought. "Oh, umm..." She knew where to find Alex's office, where to find Trina's office and the cleaning crew's breakroom, but everything else was starting to get fuzzy. "Actually, if you're not busy, would you mind giving me a quick rundown of the building?"

Trina lit up. "Oh, of course! I'd be happy to. I know it's a lot to take in, and I'm sure Alex rushed through it a bit."

"O-oh, it's not like that."

Trina scoffed. "Don't worry, that's just what Alex is like. Always rushing from one thing to the next."

Isla nodded. "Yeah, that does sound about right."

Trina hopped up and dusted herself off before gesturing for Isla to follow along. "Come with me then, we can take our time. Just let me know whenever you want to head home."

"Okay! T-thank you!" Isla added quickly, stumbling after her boss.

Trina took her through the first few floors, taking time to walk through each hallway and pointing out any of the important rooms that Isla would need to be aware of. This time, Isla took notes, making sure she remembered how to get where.

"Are there maps on the floors? What if a client comes in and I need to direct them?"

Fortunately for Isla, there were maps, but they were a bit out of the way at times, so she was grateful to have Trina to point them out to her.

"By the way," Trina asked slowly. "How do you know Ms. Chapman, if you don't mind me asking? You two seem pretty close."

Isla startled. "O-oh! Nothing too crazy, really. My sister and Alex have been friends for years. They met way back in college."

Trina looked surprised, maybe even a bit impressed too. "Wow, that's a long time. Ms. Chapman keeps to herself a lot, so no one really gets to hear about her personal life."

"You're not gonna ask me to spill the tea on her, are you?" Isla asked with a slight tease, though a small part of her wondered how many people would judge her for getting the job just because she knew Alex personally. But wasn't that how a lot of jobs worked these days? You had to network and get to know people if you even wanted a chance in the first place so this really wasn't that different, right?

"Of course not, dear!" Trina exclaimed. "I'm sorry if I made you think otherwise. Ms. Chapman is just an...anomaly of sorts. Not sure if that's the right word for it, but she's pretty private. Makes people like me curious, but that's all."

Isla nodded along. "Oh, good. Yeah, I can understand that. I honestly don't know, um, Ms. Chapman, that well myself. I hope that changes though." Isla beamed.

"Well, if anyone has a chance of getting through her tough skin, it's a cutie like you."

Isla blushed. "O-oh, thank you."

Trina winked at her. "Don't mention it."

Isla smiled politely.

"And here we are at the main break room! There's a small fridge in the custodial break room, but this room has everything you'll need. Ms. Chapman made sure everyone working here would have a good break space, which I know I appreciate."

Isla took in the room, nodding and smiling at how neat and inviting everything looked. The room curved a bit, following swirling patterns in the floor and ceiling. It felt almost like a fancy

3
ALEX CHAPMAN

Alex had never worried about keeping her office absolutely pristine, but now that Isla was going to be working for her, she figured she should be a bit more conscious of what needed cleaning. After brushing a finger across it, Alex realized the shelves definitely needed dusting, and with how chaotic her organization system was, Alex thought having a second set of eyes, hands, and a creative mind could help get things in order. Plus, it was always nice to have good company once in a while, even if Isla didn't say much. None of the other cleaners talked to her much either, other than Trina, but they were pleasant people and she enjoyed getting to know them when she had the chance.

Isla, however, was someone she knew. Yet at the same time, Alex wondered how well she really knew her. In some ways, she seemed like a complete stranger. Isla had been fairly shy in her youth, but they'd still had a few conversations here and there, even if those conversations hadn't been particularly long or deep. She wouldn't complain at the chance to have a few more interactions, or even just to see her cute face regularly.

Thankfully, Trina had already been impressed with Isla and her dedication to the job. She seemed to be exactly what Sarah had said—a good worker, sweet and lovely to get along with, and never one to complain.

Alex chuckled to herself, settling on a meeting time with a potential high-end client while she looked over the agenda once more. She finished compiling the necessary documents and checked the time, happy to find that it would be the perfect time to take her lunch.

The kitchen and company break room was a couple floors down from Alex's office, but it was always nice to get a walk in, however short it may be.

Upon arriving, Alex found the area somewhat empty. There were a few employees scattered around the room, a quiet chatter here and there, but otherwise it seemed that most people had yet to take their lunch for the day.

Alex hummed to herself as she went to retrieve her lunch. As she stepped around the corner, Alex found Isla straining to reach one of the higher cupboards. With a sigh and a cheeky smile, Alex stepped up behind her and reached up to grab down a plate. She didn't notice how close she was until she looked down, barely an inch or two away from Isla as she was pressed against the counter, still turning to face Alex with a startled expression on her face.

"Is this what you needed?" Alex asked with a soft laugh, taking a step back and handing the plate to Isla.

Isla turned with a soft blush in her cheeks, smiling that sweet little smile of hers. "Oh, yes! Thank you, Alex."

"No problem." Alex grinned, taking a moment to observe Isla's dark curly hair. It was pulled back into a thick ponytail today, as opposed to when she wore it down the day before. Her face was quite soft-looking as well, with a warm countenance and bangs that shaded her eyes, of which, Alex found to be particularly lovely.

Alex had never really taken the time to notice Isla's eyes before, but they were a deep brown, nearly black, and they seemed to practically suck you into a world of clarity and calm. They were doe-like and sweet, especially alongside her shy blush.

"Wow..." Alex stated, "Your eyes are so lovely!"

Isla's blush grew, and she pushed a strand of hair out of her eyes with her free hand as she shrugged. "Oh, they're just brown. Nothing special. You're making me blush!"

Alex hummed, resting her hand against the counter as Isla shrunk back against it. "Sorry, I don't mean to be inappropriate, even though I've known you for so long and have never mentioned it before, but your eyes just struck me."

Isla giggled as she shrunk back shyly. Her laugh was joyful and light, just like Christmas bells. "It's not inappropriate, I like it."

Without thinking much of the action, Alex reached out to tilt Isla's chin up ever so slightly by her knuckle, observing her eyes for a moment longer. "Yeah, I'd say they're pretty special. Don't sell yourself short, or perhaps, I'll have to remind you every now and again..." Alex raised a brow.

Isla seemed to get the tease, or perhaps just the flirting behind it, because her cheeks were growing to crimson red. "Remind me of what?"

"Of how lovely you are," Alex grinned playfully.

Somehow, Isla blushed even more. "Gosh, Alex," she mumbled with a small smile. "It's my first day and you're already like this? What would Sarah say?" She smirked with a sarcastic tone.

Alex smiled, rolled her eyes and opened her mouth to speak, but a figure passed by her before she had the chance.

"Sorry, I just need to get past you there," a man on the graphic design team said while stepping past them.

"No problem." Alex shrugged, looking back to Isla with a softer smile now. "Sarah would agree with me that you look even nicer than the decor around here that I picked out myself. But I guess we'll have to catch up more later then?"

Isla nodded, and Alex gave her a quick pat on the shoulder before heading off to find her lunch.

∽

Alex had to admit she was a bit distracted with work after running into Isla again. She really was quite cute, but a part of her wondered about what Isla had said. What would Sarah say? Sarah had asked Alex to take care of Isla, but never really expanded on what that might entail. Alex had wondered on a few occasions what Isla was really like behind that shy mask of hers, but she'd never had the chance, or the time, to find out. Now that Isla was here, it felt like the perfect time to get to know her better, but just from a couple interactions, Alex could clearly tell that Isla was one hundred percent her type...

Alex shook her head, pulling herself back into her work, only to be faced with a ringing cell phone in her pocket.

She answered without thinking, only to find her mother on the other line.

"Alex, dear, how are you?"

Alex's face fell, her hand automatically tensing up around the phone. "Fine. How are you?" she replied flatly.

"Well, considering your father has taken me to Greece for the week, I'm doing quite well! He says hello."

Alex took in a short breath, putting on a pained

smile as she leaned back in the chair. "Good, good. Hello to him too. Hope you both have fun—"

"We would have taken you with us, you know." Alex's mom interrupted. "But you're so busy with work and so far away, I thought it'd be too much of a hassle for you."

"Too far away?" Alex asked, voice raising slightly. "You're in Greece and you think your daughter who lives two states away is too far away?"

"Oh honey, I'm sure we can arrange something if you really want to make the trip."

Alex scoffed, "Of course I don't want to make the trip. I'm not going to travel all that way only for you to berate me for my career again."

Alex's mom sighed over the phone, her voice tinted with contempt as she spoke. "You know how I feel about your career. I put everything in place so that you could have a respectable career, like your father."

"My father who only became a doctor because he was pushed into it? That's what you want for me too, huh?" Alex rolled her eyes. "Not surprised."

"He wasn't pushed into it; he loves his work

and it's helped us all so much in life. I wouldn't have had it any other way," Alex's mom retorted.

"Ugh," Alex grumbled, pressing the heel of her hand against her brow in agitation, "I can't do this right now, Mom, I have work to do."

"Oh? Well, if you're going to be so short with me, will you at least consider doing something more meaningful with your job?"

"It's plenty meaningful!" Alex said, exasperated.

Alex's mom seemed to grimace through the phone. "That's not what I meant, dear. Just that... artwork is a wonderful career to pursue, when done in the right way—"

"Mom, I'm 47!" Alex was starting to shout. "For the last time, stop nitpicking my career! It's far too late for that, okay? I'm far more successful than you'll ever be, anyway!"

Alex hung up the call before her mom had a chance to reply.

"Ugh!!" Alex groaned, leaning back in her chair and pushing a hand through her hair. "Why is she like this?" she mumbled to herself.

After a few minutes of careful, calming breaths, Alex put her eyes back to the screen and looked over her remaining calendar items for the day.

She'd rather think about anything that wasn't her mom right now, even if that was reviewing a dull financial sheet from Jordan.

It wasn't long before Alex got her mind moving on work again and pushing through her more dull and dreary items of business gave her time to start on a new design that she'd been looking forward to. She'd just finished some initial brainstorming sketches when she heard a knock at the door.

Alex sat up straight, setting her sketchbook to the side. "Come in!"

Very slowly, the door swung open to reveal a shy, smiling Isla dressed in a pale blue button-up blouse and black jeans. Her hair was up again, and she even gave Alex a small wave as she entered. "Hello, Alex."

"Isla!" Alex's face softened, leaning forward in her chair to usher her inside. "Can I do anything for you?" Seeing Isla was a welcome relief after having to speak with her mother all of a sudden. Alex was already trying to think of something she could have Isla help with to keep her there just a touch longer, enough for Alex to calm down and take in the peaceful air that always surrounded her.

Isla shut the door behind her, taking a few

steps inside, but notably not taking the chair. She shook her head. "No, I honestly just wanted to come and formally thank you."

Alex shook her head with a laugh. "Whatever for? It's only your first day."

"Well, I think you deserve some thanks for that at least." Isla smiled sweetly. "I know you probably didn't want to take someone on out of the blue, but I think I'm really gonna like it here, and it's already been a huge help to Sarah and Mom and I."

"Of course." Alex moved to stand up from her chair.

"Oh, no, you don't need to get up or anything." Isla waved her hands in front of her in protest.

Alex carefully sat back down.

"That's all I needed." Isla spoke a bit softer, glancing behind Alex's desk as she lowered her hands and pulled at the cuffs on her sleeves. "And to grab your trash."

Alex scooted her chair to the side, gesturing behind her with a smile and a nod. "Feel free."

Isla stepped forward to grab the trash behind Alex, quickly moving to place the bag by the closed door. Alex watched as she took off her gloves and stuffed them in the trash bag as well, reaching up to carefully pull her hair tie out as she effortlessly fixed her ponytail to catch a few more stray hairs. With a sigh, she began to turn back around, and Alex couldn't help it as her eyes promptly trailed down and back up Isla's figure. Even in jeans and a casual blouse, she looked absolutely perfect. Her curvacious figure. Her deep brown eyes. Alex couldn't shake this girl out of her mind already.

Isla met Alex's gaze as she turned around, blushing ever so slightly as Alex grinned. "Have I told you how beautiful your hair is? It frames your cute face so nicely."

Again, Isla was adorably flustered at the compliment, reaching up to cover one of her blushing cheeks. "Thank you. I've always thought my hair was too wild." She shrugged.

"Psshh." Alex waved her hand in the air. "It's beautiful. There is nothing wrong with wild."

Isla shrunk behind her hand, but Alex still caught the hint of a smile. With a start, Isla looked back down at the trash bag and quickly back to Alex. "Oh, Trina told me there's one under your desk you always forget."

Alex's eyes widened in recognition and she nodded. "That's right. Come here, it's just on my right."

Isla was quick to step up to Alex's side, and God, she was even cuter up close. Isla glanced her way, the blush from earlier staining her cheeks the longer she locked eyes with Alex. Before long, she leaned down to peek under the desk, but Alex caught her arm, moving without even thinking. She couldn't stop the overwhelming desire she felt.

"O-oh!" Isla was surprised by the sudden movement, eyes darting toward Alex once more.

Before she had a chance to open her mouth, Alex pulled Isla closer. Isla's free arm reached out to catch herself against the chair as she nearly fell into Alex's lap, but Alex pulled her in. Isla leaned close hungrily as their lips joined in a soft kiss.

The kiss stifled a gasp from Isla, melding it into a sweet moan as Alex went in deep with longing, pulling at Isla's sweet, rosy lips as her hand slid to the back of Isla's neck to coax her in deeper.

Isla was startled, but she kissed back harder, leaning closer into Alex, who felt a stirring of want within her.

As Isla leaned in, Alex pushed back, slowly rising to her feet and taking hold of Isla by her side, stepping her forward into the desk behind her. Their lips parted in a sharp gasp, but Alex hummed against Isla and pressed herself into her harder with a short step forward.

Isla moaned, clinging to the front of Alex's shirt as Alex slipped her tongue into their kiss. Her mind was far gone, but her heart was already screaming for more, taking taste after taste of the beautiful Isla who was all hers in that moment. The chemistry between them was palpable.

Alex hummed and pressed her palms around to Isla's back, clinging to the blouse and arching closer as she tilted her head to capture just a touch more of Isla's heavenly lips.

A small buzzing sound entered Alex's mind as she relished in a sharp whine coming from Isla through their dancing lips. The buzzing grew louder, and for a moment, Alex ignored it, moaning herself before breaking away with a series of unrelenting breaths.

Alex's eyes darted to the side where her phone lay on the desk, buzzing and tilting as the name *Sarah Hart* appeared on the screen, complete with a profile picture that was over a decade old.

"Shit, shit, shit," Alex cursed, grabbing the phone and taking a deep breath as she stepped back from Isla. A part of her considered answering the call to make the whole situation seem less suspicious than it was already growing to be, but her instincts forced her to mute her phone and set it down. She'd call her back later. There was no way Sarah had any idea of what had just occurred anyway.

With another long breath, Alex turned her gaze to Isla, who was still panting and stuck against the desk with a face as red as cherries.

"Sorry," Alex whispered on instinct, pulling Isla out of her stunned silence.

"W-what?"

Alex cleared her throat, urging her heart to settle. "I'm...I'm sorry." Alex took another deep breath.

"For...for kissing me?" Isla's face contorted in a mixture of confusion, bliss, embarrassment, and shock.

Alex nodded. "Yes," she sighed. "Damn, I really shouldn't have done that. You are my best friend's sister and I do not think she'd approve," Alex said while taking another step back into her chair, which she readily flopped into with a grunt.

"But? Then why did you?"

Alex waved the question away. "I shouldn't have, and that's all that matters. You're very cute,

Isla, but that was far too inappropriate for me to do as your boss, let alone as your sister's friend."

Isla's face quickly fell from its expression of bliss, nodding carefully.

"I'm sorry. We should both get back to work and forget about this. Here," Alex said while reaching under her desk to grab the trash bin, heart still hammering from the way she wanted to pull Isla back in despite her mind bringing reason back to the forefront.

Isla took the trash bin with a soft nod, taking and replacing the bag without a word. She handed it back to Alex and quickly turned to head out.

"Isla—" Alex began, surprising herself as the name escaped her lips.

Isla turned, and Alex wasn't sure whether the red in Isla's cheeks was from the kiss or the consequences of it.

"Feel free to take off early if you'd like," Alex offered softly. "Tell Trina I said it was fine."

Isla nodded, offering a near-silent, "O-okay," as she left the room, leaving Alex in a sudden and startlingly anxious sense of uncertainty.

∼

The rest of Alex's day at the office was filled with distractions. She entered meetings with anxious threads rising up within her, only to be pushed aside as she busied herself in work. She walked through the main office, talking with coworkers and checking on projects that she'd nearly forgotten about. And she decided not to call Sarah back, instead choosing to wait until the workday was over, for better or for worse.

Once she was in the safety of her home, however, Alex had nothing to distract her from the guilt pricking at her from inside. Normally, she'd be able to brush off a kiss in the moment like it was nothing, but this was different. This was Isla. This was Sarah's sister. And if Sarah found out...

"Gosh, she really doesn't need anymore stress on her plate right now," Alex groaned, sliding down in her chair.

Alex had her phone in hand and checked the missed call from Sarah. There was no voicemail, no text, so apparently, it wasn't important.

Alex sighed.

After a moment of contemplation, Alex sent a quick text.

Sorry, busy with work. What's up?

She watched the text for a moment longer, but

she knew better than to expect an immediate reply from Sarah. Instead, she pulled up Isla's contact in her phone.

Alex grimaced as she contemplated hitting the call button. Trying to just ignore the situation was only going to make things worse. If not for her, it would be for Isla, and she didn't deserve that.

Alex pressed the call button, waiting for a few rings before Isla answered. "Hello? May I ask who this is?"

"Hi Isla," Alex began, putting on the sweetest voice she could muster. "It's Alex, I got your number from work, but I wanted to talk to you about earlier, if you have a second."

Isla paused for a moment, then Alex caught traces of footsteps and a door being shut before Isla responded in a hushed and careful tone, "I, um... I have a second."

Alex grimaced. Clearly this was already taking a toll on Isla. "Hey, I'm sorry. I really am," Alex sighed.

"I know," Isla mumbled. "I'm... I'm sorry too."

"Isla, you have nothing to be sorry for. I made a move on you and that's my fault. I just wanted to make things right and make some things clear moving forward. Does that sound alright?"

Isla took a moment to respond, but she replied with a soft, "It does."

Alex sighed in relief, gathering her thoughts before speaking carefully. "How I acted today will have no affect on your job, I can assure you of that. You still have the job, and you're free to continue as you wish, or not if you'd prefer, but I know that's not really an option for you right now."

Isla hummed a soft no through the phone.

"I'm sorry for how I acted, and for leading you on. But as I'm sure you know, we'll still be working in close quarters at times, and in order for that to continue... What I did can't happen again." Isla was quiet on the other line, so hastily, Alex added, "It *won't* happen again."

Again, it took Isla a few moments to respond, but her quiet voice came through the line loud and clear. "Okay. I understand. I'm still sorry, too, for my part in not stopping it."

Alex bit back a retort that Isla really didn't need to apologize. Deep down, Alex knew Isla was aware of that. She took a slow breath and nodded. "Okay. We're good then, Isla? I still want us to be friends, and for you to feel safe and happy while working here. I just want to say I'm really sorry I crossed that boundary with you. It was utterly unprofessional of me."

"Thank you, I appreciate that," Isla replied softly.

Alex nodded, but it was more to herself than to Isla. There was a brief moment where Alex wasn't quite sure what to say, but after just long enough for the awkwardness of their situation to settle in, Alex figured it was time to leave things be for the night. "Alright. I'll see you tomorrow then. Have a nice night, Isla."

"You too, Alex. Thank you."

Alex hung up the call and set her phone to the side, closing her eyes and processing the day with a drawn-out sigh. The guilt sinking into the corners of her heart was still there, but less present now. Setting boundaries and making things right was the best she could do after something like that. She sighed again, looking at the clock. Taking an early night might not be a bad idea to get her back on track for tomorrow. She had lots to think about, and if she was being honest, she'd much rather not. Leave the thinking to her dreams and the action for tomorrow—where things could simply return to normal.

4

ISLA HART

Alex's lips had tasted like the dazzling bonfire that was raging within her soul, and Isla had dwelled on the thought too many times than she cared to admit in the past few days. Lying in her bed at night, she replayed the moments, the touches, the kiss. She touched herself countless times just at the thought of it. The butterflies of excitement panged over her every time. Unfortunately, the thought was also tainted with regret. She hadn't even been the one to act, but still, Isla felt as if she'd done something horribly wrong. If nothing else, it had been a moment that felt extraordinarily right that she would never, ever, have again.

On Isla's first day back, the wound was still fresh. She tried to convince herself that the experience was a dream. She tried to avoid Alex as much as possible, but any moment she caught a glimpse of Alex's striking eyes, her heart raced faster than a hummingbird's wings, and that made her mess of emotions even worse.

Her second day back, Isla had the chance to spend the whole day cleaning up the breakroom, and she immediately took it. Trina's chatter and advice was a welcome distraction, but not enough to last once Isla came across files and supplies, and even some old graphic design work, with Alex's name all over it.

It was Isla's fourth day back now, and things hadn't gotten much better. Any interactions with Alex were brief and stunted, and Isla had to stop herself a number of times when a flirty comment or a tiny compliment popped into her head. Even if she was just being nice, Alex might not take it that way. She'd been very clear that they couldn't be anything more, and Isla didn't want to chance upsetting her boss and friend. Although, it was getting harder and harder to see them as friends. She was doing everything in her power to avoid

Alex and the awkward air between them, and she wouldn't be surprised if Alex was doing the same.

That morning, Alex had asked Isla to organize some of her older files, so Isla took a cart full of files to Trina's office to prevent any more awkwardness by working in the same room as Alex for so long. Many of the files were designs and sketches that had long been changed or approved or simply forgotten. Isla was pleasantly surprised when she came across a few clothing designs.

"Well, well, well...the great Alex Chapman wanted to be a clothing designer at some point?" she chuckled to herself, taking a moment to appreciate the sketches of dazzling dresses and jackets and shawls and more, before setting them aside to file in the miscellaneous folder.

She found a few more old designs and wondered if Alex had ever made anything of the designs or if they'd been pushed aside in favor of what Chapman Signature Studios had become.

The next file wasn't a file at all, but in fact, a photo of Alex about 10 years prior. "Wow…" Isla stared, noting Alex's former curls falling to the side of her strong jawline. "Now, *that's* the Alex I remember." But not everything was the same. Alex had an undercut in this image, and her outfit was much more professional than what she tended to wear nowadays. Isla assumed Alex had always been confident enough to wear whatever she wanted, but maybe there was a time when Alex was a bit new to all this herself and had to dress the part in order for people to take her seriously. Even so, Isla couldn't help but think how good Alex looked in a suit.

Isla glanced at the clock as she finally tore her eyes from the picture, but she must have been staring longer than she'd realized.

"Damn, it's been an hour already?"

"Since you started, yes," Trina mumbled from her desk, not even glancing up from her paperwork.

Isla was quick to apologize and decided it was time she worked double-time to make up for the distraction.

When she finally made it back to Alex's office thirty minutes later, it was empty, and Isla let out a sigh of relief. Her hammering heart slowly settled down as she put the files back in place, taking care to use this golden opportunity to grab any trash before she left.

Isla thought about checking the main office and hallway for signs of Alex before she stepped out, but if Alex was there, Isla was sure she'd look incredibly stupid while trying to so obviously avoid her. So instead, she put on her best smile and slipped out the door, only to bump right into a tall woman in a silky black blouse.

"Oh, Isla?" Alex mumbled in confusion.

"Sorry!" Isla whispered, ducking behind Alex and out the door before she could start a conversation.

"It's no problem." Alex blinked. "Thanks for the help."

Isla gave her boss a nod before swiftly turning on her heel and heading back to Trina's office, mortified at the startling blush on her face.

Just seeing Alex was bad enough but running into her was even worse. It felt stupid to think that Alex's hand simply brushing against her arm was enough to remind Isla of their kiss, that catching her eye for one split second was enough for her to wish she could collapse into Alex's strong arms and let Alex hold her close. Plus, she was wearing that same enticing perfume than pulled Isla's heart into a knot of want.

Before seeing Trina again, Isla stopped in the restroom and made sure the blush in her cheeks had died down. At this rate, maybe she'd need to start caking on foundation to try and hide it.

"No, no, that's stupid," Isla berated herself, sighing and rubbing her face as she forced herself to go back to work.

When Isla glimpsed Alex getting her lunch in the break room, she felt her face light on fire once more. The black blouse she was wearing today was form-fitting and quite flattering on her, and the sharp alternating of her hips as she walked was nearly impossible to tear her eyes away from. She'd never really wondered what it'd be like to have someone like Alex saunter slowly toward her with hooded eyes and a knowing smirk, but somehow the image of Alex herself doing that was all Isla could play in her mind as she watched from afar, dreaming that the fantasy would end in a kiss…and maybe something more.

After taking her own lunch break, Isla did everything in her power to keep busy, but before long, that included working in Alex's office again. Alex needed some dusting done, and then she was to vacuum the floors.

When she stepped inside, Isla half-expected Alex to stand up and saunter over to her, just like she'd imagined, but her boss hardly gave Isla a glance before pointing to a number of frames, trinkets, and mementos she'd piled in the corner opposite her.

"Those need dusting. You can leave them on the chair when you're done."

Isla nodded, a bit deflated. "Will do, Alex."

Alex paused in her work. "It's um..." Alex started, twirling her tablet pen lazily in the air. "It's probably for the best if you call me Ms. Chapman or Ma'am. At least while you're at work."

"Oh..." Isla's face fell completely. She turned away before Alex could sneak a look at her face. "You're right, that's probably for the best....ma'am."

Referring to Alex in such a formal way felt beyond foreign, but Isla stepped over to the corner to start dusting anyway, waiting in the silence for a response, or maybe an apology, but none came. All she could hear was the near-silent scratching of Alex drawing on her tablet, and the periodic streams of typing followed by soft sighs of exhaustion settling in. She didn't enjoy this ice queen role which Alex could so easily adopt. She knew there was a very different person behind that mask, but she didn't know if she could melt the ice to uncover it.

Isla was fairly certain the silence wasn't

because Alex was mad at her, but she couldn't help entertaining it as a possibility. Alex just wanted to keep things professional, and if Isla really thought about it, this wasn't much different to other cleaning jobs she'd taken. It was nice to talk to the staff, but a lot of them just ignored her. Usually, they were all busy and tired enough, Isla included, but it had been nice to have a few days without that silence. She had hoped it would last a bit longer than this.

Even as Isla began vacuuming the space, Alex stayed quiet and focused on her work. Anytime Isla tried catching a glimpse of her, those stone-cold eyes were locked on the screen with a heart far, far away from her own.

By the time Isla was finishing up, Alex stepped out to meet with someone from her main marketing team, giving Isla nothing but a rushed wave and a nod, not even a smile. She didn't want to take it personally, but it was hard not to after their first day or two working together. Even without their secret kiss, she'd hoped they could still be friendly.

Isla turned off the vacuum, letting the stuttering silence and emptiness of the room envelope her for a moment. She could hear Alex chatting just outside the room. She might enter any moment, breaking the still moment of near silence that Isla wanted to hold onto for just a moment more. One moment passed, then two, then Isla sighed and began gathering her supplies before returning back to Trina for her next assignment.

∽

Rhonda, one of Alex's assistants, was leaving, and Isla felt bummed that she'd never had the chance to meet her. Most of the office had been at her farewell party that afternoon, but Isla didn't even know it was going on until Trina asked her to clean it up.

Isla didn't really know what went on in these types of office parties, but the main office was a bit of a mess when she finally arrived. There had certainly been food and drinks, perhaps a couple games. Isla wondered if any of the cleaning crew were invited and she hadn't been told because she was new. Or perhaps, it was a smaller gathering, just a few friends that had somehow made a mess fit for dozens of people. Isla sighed.

A couple stragglers were helping to stack or move chairs, or at least make sure most of the trash was in the bins, but they didn't stay long. Isla greeted them all with a smile while they thanked her, heading off for their offices or homes while Isla surveyed the mess before her.

Luckily, whoever had organized the event had put any leftover food away, so Isla only had to deal with some empty boxes, wrappers, plasticware, and the rest of the mess the party goers had left behind. She wanted to be annoyed at the carelessness that led to messes like these, but not many seemed to think of the custodians, janitors, and cleaners coming to tidy things up behind them. Maybe she could talk to Alex about that, but maybe not—it was her job after all. And after their current tricky relationship, Isla wasn't sure she wanted to be asking Alex for any more favors.

For a while, Isla was on her own, taking her duties one step at a time. She was hefting the trash bags to the side of the room when she noticed a figure in one of the neighboring offices. It was Alex.

Alex's office was right at the hallway entrance where the area opened up into the main office space. Her door was open, and quiet music spilled from the room. Isla was already staying late to clean up the aftermath of the party, but it looked like Alex was staying late too. Maybe she'd fallen behind due to the party, or maybe she just always stayed this late. Isla had never stopped to think about how a boss of a prestigious company would probably stay late to tidy up the work no one else was going to finish. In a strange way, it kind of felt similar to her own work as a cleaner.

After first noticing her, Isla was a bit nervous at having Alex there. There was no one else in the office, after all. But as the minutes ticked on, Isla found herself hoping more and more that Alex might be watching. From taking out the trash, to sweeping, mopping, vacuuming the floors, and more, Isla did her best to take her time, trying, but not too hard, to catch a glimpse of Alex in case her eyes were watching Isla work.

For a while, Isla stayed busy with no sign of Alex acknowledging her existence, but on her third attempt of catching a peek, she saw it—Alex ever so carefully peeking up from her work to watch Isla as she reached up toward a high shelf. As Isla glanced away, she had the distinct feeling that Alex was still watching her, eyes boring into her back and sending goosebumps down her spine. Isla was on her tiptoes, straining her arm to grab a cup still full of soda without knocking it on herself, and after a moment, she finally did. Settled back on her feet once more, Isla did start to wonder if her shirt had ridden up, and maybe that's what had caught Alex's eye.

Isla tugged her shirt down a bit as she turned about to start scrubbing at the tables, feeling her face blossom into red. She caught Alex watching a couple more times, and Isla hoped that meant Alex hadn't looked away, even as her heart went racing every time she considered the possibility that Alex's icy eyes were still studying her.

Before long, each movement felt like it was part of a dance, like she was performing on stage for an audience of one. Despite how menial her tasks were, Isla tried to perform them with grace. It almost made her want to dance, or maybe she was dancing in her own strange way, as if cleaning could somehow be made elegant or graceful. She smiled and hummed comfortably to the pinpricks of music coming from Alex's office, knowing she was too far to actually hear Isla hum along.

The work started to go much faster at that, and Isla even found herself twirling around here and there. Isla smiled as she worked, making her dance something of a game. By pretending to make something so dull so fun, it was starting to feel that way, and it was made even easier knowing she had an audience.

Isla hummed more, closing her eyes at times and cleaning by memory. She scrubbed at everything in the room until it shone, exhausted, but more than proud of the work she'd accomplished.

However, the next time Isla tried to catch a glimpse of Alex, she was gone. The faint music had long since stopped, the office was empty, yet clean, and Isla was dancing all on her own.

Isla's face fell as she looked about, letting out a slow and sorrowful breath. She felt her cheeks warm once more, more embarrassed at being caught by no one than being caught by Alex.

"Oh..." Isla whispered in defeat. "Guess that's that," she mumbled, sluggishly grabbing hold of her last few cleaning supplies and setting them on her cart. "Time to head home."

Isla took another moment to glance back at Alex's office, but it was still empty and still quiet. She took her time in putting everything away, making certain that all the supplies were exactly where she found them. For a brief moment, Isla was proud of herself once more for being able to navigate the building so easily after only a couple days of working, but that thought quickly fled as

5
ALEX CHAPMAN

Alex didn't like to admit how often she stayed at work late. It was a habit she was trying to fix, but farewell parties and work trainings and the like made it more and more difficult to get her work done by the time evening came. However, she could make an exception for this last farewell party.

Rhonda had been her assistant for many years, and though Alex was sad to see her go, Rhonda had secured her dream job, something Alex wasn't going to stand in the way of. She was happy for her, and with Isla's recent help, Alex didn't think she'd even need to hire another assistant anytime soon.

The party was a rousing success, with plenty of food and drinks and games. Alex let her professional face fall for a bit to enjoy herself, but by the end, she was able to bring everyone back together to tidy up a bit and travel home safely.

Alex hadn't considered how much of a mess they left behind until she noticed Isla in the main office. She hadn't expected anyone else to be here after the party, and if there had been custodians cleaning up after past parties, she hadn't really noticed.

Isla was scrubbing the carpet with a grimace on her face. Alex didn't know they'd spilled anything to cause such a stain, but with a closer look, she noticed several stains, as well as crumbs, leftover plates piled high in the trash, and a few on the floor as well. Maybe they hadn't tidied up as well as she'd thought.

Alex noticed Isla rising to her feet, so she quickly pulled her eyes back to her work. She didn't want to make things more uncomfortable than they already were for the poor girl. Alex still had plenty to do herself. Isla would finish up quick and head home, and that would be that.

But she didn't head home quick. Every time Alex glanced up, Isla was still working. First, she was scrubbing the carpets, then picking up debris and bagging up the trash, then scrubbing down the tables and polishing them till they shone. At one point, Isla took off her gloves to push her sleeves up and tie up her hair, revealing a set of slender arms with more muscle on them than Alex had first thought.

"Hmm..." Alex hummed to herself, resting her head on her closed hand as she tapped her pen on the desk and watched Isla work.

Isla wasn't particularly muscular, but she was certainly fit and pleasing to the eye. That, combined with her more petite frame, made her look like a little angel flitting to and fro amidst her cleaning supplies. Probably not the image most people would think of when they saw someone cleaning, but Isla managed to move with grace through every moment Alex had eyes on her. She wondered what Isla would have been like during her most successful times as a dancer. Although, she'd never confirmed with Isla herself if that was something she still pursued today, perhaps she still did.

At one point, Alex tried to look back at the document she hadn't touched in several minutes, but her eyes were drawn right back up to Isla stretching up on her tiptoes to reach one of the top shelves in the main office. Her shirt rode up just enough to reveal her shapely waist, arching upward as she leaned onto one foot and let the other float in the air, as if she was actually dancing.

Alex chuckled to herself. *God, she is too cute.* For a moment, Alex thought Isla might have looked her way, but she was back to work before long, so Alex figured she'd let herself enjoy the show.

Isla continued moving about with a practiced ease. She even hummed a little to the soft music Alex was playing as mere background noise. Alex did think it was a shame that Isla wore more loose clothes to work, but it made sense for her position and even gave Alex the chance to linger in her own imagination. She couldn't help but look in Isla's direction.

Alex slowly became transfixed with Isla's bouncing curls and her warm lips stretched into a smile; the bunching muscles in her arms and shoulders as she worked—her softly-heaving chest, and her dainty, but strong, little hands.

The longer Alex watched, the more she wished that their kiss could have lasted just a bit longer. If she'd known she would come to her senses and cut the whole thing off after the fact, maybe Alex would have done a bit more, perhaps kissed Isla elsewhere, let her hands travel farther and faster before that wretched buzz of her phone broke the moment. If Isla hadn't been Sarah's sister, maybe they could have done more or simply gotten away with a little more and made this thing last beyond just a sneaky little kiss.

Isla stumbled and nearly tripped over a bottle of disinfectant, breaking the trance and pulling Alex back to reality.

"I can't be thinking like that about Sarah's sister..." Alex mumbled, watching just a second more before she looked down at her tablet.

She'd barely made any progress since Isla had arrived, and she likely wouldn't do much more if she stuck around. Even if the thought made her grimace, it was probably for the best if she just headed home.

Alex quickly and quietly packed up her belongings and set everything in her office back in its place; she'd become quite practiced in packing up quickly and getting out of the office in a rush. She grabbed her bag and slung it on her shoulder, staring through the open doorway at a very focused and hard-at-work Isla. Her hair was slowly coming out of her ponytail, but she brushed it to the side and kept on working. Alex was startled by how much she wanted to brush the hair out of Isla's face herself, running her hands through her gorgeous curls and all over her perfect body.

Alex blinked herself back to reality before turning away and slipping out the building, away from Isla's line of sight, letting go of the fantasy. She sighed as she walked in silence, pressing the heel of her hand into her brow to pull herself out of those carnal thoughts.

Alex hated being so cold with Isla. She'd told her they could still be friends, and she, of course, wanted that, but her heart wanted so much more, and she just didn't trust it right now. It was taking a toll on Isla though. She was more and more awkward in every interaction, and those seemed to be happening less and less in the first place. Maybe it was a mistake for Alex to keep her working close by after their kiss. But on the other hand, maybe it would be worse for her to push Isla away. Doing so might even push Sarah out of her life, too.

With a groan, Alex slid into her car, slumping in the seat and letting every ounce of her CEO mannerisms fade away. Isla was uncomfortable with the distance, that much was obvious. But beyond that, Alex didn't really know Isla all that well. All the times they'd interacted over the years had been brief and inconsequential. Isla had always been too busy working, or spending time with friends, or taking care of her mom. Both she and Sarah were always good about doing that: taking care of each other, keeping their family together. Alex didn't want to come between them, but it was getting harder and harder to get Isla out of her head. She hadn't thought much of it, and even though Alex always thought Isla was pretty cute, she had never even been on the table before since she was Sarah's little sister.

Alex sat back up in her seat, turning the car on and staring out into the dark, empty sky. Isla was Sarah's little sister, but surely she was still her own person too. Alex had taken full responsibility for making a move that day, and she still did, but Isla still had a say in how things moved forward, even if Alex didn't care to admit it. Maybe she was the one letting personal things take charge of her work life by not even interacting with Isla in a way that gave her any sort of chance. Alex really did want to make sure Isla felt safe, and hopefully happy, while she was there, but maybe it would take more than just keeping distance to make that happen.

Her mind kept circling on what to do the whole way home. Once she got settled inside, she made herself a cup of tea and settled down onto the couch, trying to open up a book, but she still couldn't focus. Her eyes glazed over the page, thinking of nothing, then thinking of work, then thinking of Isla. The guilt of making Isla feel so out of place kept creeping back into Alex's heart, not even trying to work from home could keep her mind off of it.

After attempting to distract herself on her phone for a few dull minutes, Alex finally gave in and opened up her contacts. Already up was Isla's contact from a few days ago when Alex had called her last. Alex sighed, slightly annoyed at herself for not calling anyone else in that time. Or maybe Isla was just on her mind so much that Alex kept going back to it without even realizing.

"God, I really need to get these feelings under control," Alex muttered as she hit the call button before she circled through her train of thought once more. She didn't know exactly what to say to make things right, but surely something was better than nothing at this point, right?

The phone rang several times before Isla's

sweet and soft voice picked up with a tentative, "Hello?"

"Hi, Isla, it's Alex."

"Oh, um, did you need something? I was just about to leave the office," Isla replied quickly, sounding hushed and almost nervous.

"Nothing like that, Isla," Alex began cheerfully. "I honestly just wanted to apologize for how I've been acting the past few days. I know I've been a bit distant, as I'm sure you've noticed..." Alex paused, playing out the right words in her head before letting out a soft, "I'm...I'm sorry."

Isla took a moment to reply, but she seemed as cheerful and sweet as ever. "I mean, it's not a problem. I figured things might be a little different between us," Isla said slowly, growing calmer in her tone. "It might just take some time."

Alex bit her lip to stop herself from a quick reply. Isla had clearly been upset the past few days, or at the very least, uncomfortable with the situation. But Alex didn't want to make assumptions either. The more she thought about it, the more she realized how little she knew of Isla, or even just how to read her.

"You're right, it will take time, I think." Alex smiled through the phone. "But that doesn't mean

I don't want to try now. How about you swing by on your way home from work for a quick treat? My house is on the way, right?"

Alex heard a small, startled sound from the other line. "Come to your house? I wouldn't want to intrude! Plus, it's getting late…"

"Nonsense! I'd love to have you over," Alex insisted, a strange excitement bubbling up in her chest that she chose to ignore. "But only if you're comfortable with it, of course. I know I've been distant, and I'd like to change that. I'd like for us to actually be friends and feel comfortable around one another. What do you say? Let me make it up to you."

It sounded like Isla was about to start a sentence, but then she stopped herself. It took her another moment to respond, returning right back to that sweet, soft, and calming voice. "I'd like that, too. For us to still be friends. I probably can't stay for long, but I can stop by if you're sure it's no trouble. I'd really like to let go of this frosty atmosphere between us."

For some reason, Alex couldn't help but grin from ear to ear at the response. "It's no trouble at all, I promise. You're just a few minutes away, right? Text me if there's anything I can get ready for you

—a drink, a cup of tea, or anything else. Drive safe!"

"T-thank you!" Isla stumbled back quietly. "I, um...I guess I'll be there soon!"

Alex hung up and leaned back against her couch with a sneaking smile spreading across her face. The idea of having Isla over at her house was thrilling, in a way. A part of her was desperate to have some alone time with the sweet girl, but Alex hoped that, at least for now, this would be a good chance to talk and make things right. Hopefully, they could both leave feeling better about the situation and their friendship moving forward. She could do this, and she *wanted* to do this, for herself, for Sarah, and for sweet Isla.

∼

By the time Alex heard a knock at the door, she had mugs of herbal tea steeping for the both of them.

"Come in, Isla!" Alex said with a grin, opening the door and ushering Isla inside.

Isla was wearing a large maroon coat on top of her outfit from work. She gave Alex a shy smile.

"Thank you for inviting me. Sorry I'm just in my work clothes—"

"Oh, you're fine!" Alex interrupted, leading Isla to the couch with her hand barely brushing against the small of her back. "I was the one who invited you to come straight from work anyway." Alex pulled her hand away, offering it to Isla. "May I take your coat?"

Isla blinked. "Oh, sure. Thank you."

Alex took the coat and hung it up. "You said you liked lavender tea, right?"

"Mm hmm," Isla hummed in reply, her hands bunched up atop her legs once she set herself down on the couch.

Alex hoped she hadn't been too forward in inviting Isla over. She seemed nervous, but maybe she just needed a chance to open up and relax a little first. "Just one moment then, let me bring them over."

Alex disappeared into the kitchen for a minute, quickly adding a bit of honey to Isla's cup, as she was fairly sure that's what she liked.

When Alex returned to the living room, Isla hadn't moved an inch, turning to give Alex another nervous smile. It was by far time for Alex to get that girl out of her shell.

"Here you are." Alex handed her the mug, plopping down on the couch right next to Isla. "Oh, sorry," she mumbled as she watched Isla's tea slosh around in her mug, but she managed to keep from spilling and gave Alex a quick, shy smile instead.

Alex watched as Isla took a sip and pulled away with a blossoming smile on her face. She turned to face Alex, already growing more relaxed than before.

"That's delicious, it's very sweet! Just how I like it."

Alex smiled. "That's what I thought. Glad I guessed right."

Slowly, Isla seemed to let herself relax into the couch, taking small sips that brought the warmth back to her eyes and cheeks. "You just guessed? Do you not make yours this way?"

"Oh, hell no." Alex rolled her eyes. "Try mine."

Isla set her cup down to take a quick sip of Alex's. She handed the mug over while mumbling, "Be warned, you won't like it."

Isla's face scrunched up as she handed the mug back. "You're right. That's almost... Well, it's just bitter."

Alex took a careful swig of her drink. "Just how I like it."

Isla giggled a bit at that, covering her mouth with the most adorable little white gloves.

"What are these?" Alex whispered, reaching out to take hold of Isla's hand and turn it over in her own. "They're cute, but you must be pretty warm in here."

"O-oh, um..." Isla startled, her cheeks growing pinker. "I guess so. Yeah, I am a little warm."

"Hmm," Alex hummed while carefully taking off the glove and setting it to the side, holding her hand out for the next one. "Why don't I help you with that?"

"You know it drives me crazy how you make me feel. Just by being next to me. Are you sure we can just be friends?" Isla sighed.

Alex quietly removed the other glove, carefully rubbing her thumb back and forth along Isla's knuckles while she felt Isla watching her with renewed curiosity. With a smirk, Alex leaned down and pressed her lips against the top of Isla's hand, lingering for a couple moments more before pulling back with a renewed spark of interest in her eyes. "Sorry, I don't know what to say. I think we could be? I'm worried Sarah would kill me if we weren't," Alex replied, trying to remind calm and collected in her response, even if she was desperate to rip her clothes off.

Isla was bright red, and her tone was wavering, but she was clearly trying to play it off. "Do you want to remove any other items of clothing?"

Alex raised a brow, squeezing Isla's hand ever so carefully.

Isla gasped, stuttering, "S-sorry, I didn't mean —I was just joking—"

"Isla," Alex shushed her with a smirk. "Don't tempt me."

While the idea of undressing *all* of Isla was becoming more and more appealing by the second, Isla was clearly pretty nervous at the idea, even if it was supposed to be "a joke." And on top of that, Alex had brought Isla here to make things right. She let go of Isla's hand.

"Sorry," Alex chuckled softly. "Before I leave you *too* speechless with my charm, I did want to ask how you've been doing at work the past few days?"

Isla nodded, turning her blushing face away to take a long sip of her tea. "I've been fine," she said softly, setting the mug back down again and bringing her gaze back to Alex with a great deal of force.

Alex scoffed, "You've *not* been fine. You get all jittery anytime you're around me. Plus, you just seem...off."

Isla looked down again, biting her lip as Alex watched with growing concern. "Like I said... I knew it'd be different, with us."

Alex nodded, stopping herself from interrupting again.

"You, um...you said it yourself; you've been distant and...a bit cold too. I just don't want to make anything worse. I can't help the feelings I get."

"Isla, dear..." Alex whispered. "You won't make it worse, that was all on me. Don't worry about it, okay?"

Isla let out a breath and nodded slowly. "I know. Easier said than done though."

"Well, you're not the only one."

Isla's brow furrowed. "What do you mean?

Alex shrugged. "I've just been worrying about too many things I shouldn't. Maybe you're rubbing off on me." Alex knocked her shoulder against Isla's with a grin.

Isla still looked pretty serious though, eyes

searching Alex's for something more. "Worrying about what?"

"Hmm..." Alex hummed, twisting in her seat on the couch to better face Isla, who somehow managed to sit up even straighter and more polite. "Well, for starters, I've been worried about you, and why the only time I've seen you dance was when no one was watching."

This time it was Isla's turn to scoff, turning away and tucking a strand of hair behind her ear as Alex leaned a touch closer. "Come on, what is it really?" she muttered with a blush in her cheeks.

"It's that, plain as day." Alex grinned. "It's so lovely to see you dance so freely, it makes me sad you won't do it more."

"Well, I can't, really. Most people would just think it's weird." Isla shrunk in on herself.

"And am I most people?" Alex asked, tilting her head to catch Isla's eye. She couldn't resist drawing her hand up to Isla's jaw, guiding her gaze up with the barest touch that sent fire blossoming in her cheeks.

Isla simply shook her head, eyes growing wide as she searched Alex's for answers.

"Happy to hear it. It was quite a treat for me to watch you..."

Isla nodded, lips twitching at a smile.

"Did you know I was watching?"

Isla looked to the side and took a careful breath before looking back at Alex. "I hoped you were."

The tiny comment brought Alex right back to a startling grin. Isla was beyond adorable, she had to be putting in a great deal of effort to make herself so irresistible.

"Are you aware of how unbelievably beautiful you are, Isla?" Alex spoke in a silky, low, and drawn-out tone.

Isla slowly shook her head.

"Or how beautiful you danced earlier...just for me?"

Isla looked down and bit her lip, but it was clear enough to Alex that she had been dancing for her. "I think I need reminding."

Isla swallowed, her shoulders scrunching up as Alex leaned in closer. Her lips parted and she let out a soft moan, meeting Alex's cool gaze with one mixed with wariness, intrigue, and want.

Alex's heart fluttered in excitement. Before she could stop herself, she hissed out low and quick, "Then dance with me, Isla." Pushing herself forward and closing the gap between them without a second thought. Her hand twisted around to cup the back of Isla's neck, pulling her in close as their lips crashed together in the start of a beautiful dance.

Isla gasped and Alex pressed in deeper, her heart pounding with excitement that was already surfacing in her hurried hands. She wasted no time in slipping a hand up the back of Isla's shirt, pulling her in so that she practically tumbled into Alex's open lap.

Their dancing lips were hurried and clumsy, but Alex didn't care, too focused on pushing and pulling against Isla's lips that were softer than they had any right to be, drawing out a startled and stunted breath with a hint of want, that before long, was slipping into a longing moan.

With her arm wrapped around Isla's back, Alex squeezed her side, causing her to flinch and fall right back into their ever-moving kiss.

Alex pulled back with a gasp, taking one heaving breath before her voice spilled out steady and deep, "Maybe it's time we get to that undressing you mentioned earlier…"

Isla sucked in a stuttering breath and dove right back in to meet Alex's lips, her hands cupping Alex's face and pulling her closer with her hands and lips and tongue.

Alex grunted, readily slipping her tongue into Isla's open and inviting mouth. The sweet girl moaned, her hands sliding down the sides of Alex's neck until she was clinging to the front of Alex's shirt.

"Are you... sure we should... do this? I thought we were trying to be friends? We could just be... casual fun?" Isla moaned.

"I can do casual fun, and all I know is how I want you so much right now. Just looking at you drives me wild," Alex whispered as she reveled in their kiss. She slid her hand up Isla's back, and she arched into Alex in return. Isla's legs, those gorgeous legs covered in far too much fabric, were shifting and wrapping themselves around Alex's waist, to which she growled, pulling back with a start to lift Isla's shirt up and over her head.

Isla's perfect body was far more pristine than she'd expected. She still had the build of a dancer, even after many years without practice. Her waist had the most subtle but elegant curve to it, with strong abdominal muscles rising and falling just below her heaving chest. Isla's black bra rose and fell with her chest, captivating Alex just long enough for Isla to reach forward and furiously begin unbuttoning the front of Alex's shirt, which sent a whole host of new feelings coursing through her body.

Before she had a chance to stop herself, Alex forced herself to her feet, taking Isla with her. Alex kept a strong hold on Isla's waist while she continued furiously going through the next few buttons. Isla's legs tightened around Alex's waist, forcing a rough groan from Alex's lips as she tangled her free hand in Isla's hair, roughly pulling her back into a quick and passionate kiss.

Alex stumbled across the living room with Isla's hands quickly finding their way inside her shirt as Alex's tongue found its way back into Isla's mouth. She stepped through the door to her bedroom, pushing it shut with her foot and collapsing to the bed just in time to throw her shirt aside.

With Isla's flushed face framed against Alex's frosty blue bedsheets, Alex let her body take control, quickly climbing atop Isla and locking her lips right in the nape of Isla's neck.

"Oh *Alex*," Isla moaned, hands sliding around Alex's sides and pulling her closer with those dainty but strong hands that wanted so much more. To which, Alex was happy to oblige.

Alex spared no time removing any remaining

items of clothing, hurling them onto the other side of the room. She pressed her hips in between Isla's legs and kissed her deeply.

"Tell me I'm not crazy; you want this just as much as me, right?" Alex asked.

"I want this more than *anything,*" Isla moaned as she dug her nails into Alex's strong back.

Without any more words, Alex kissed down Isla's soft skin, teasing her body with her tongue and lips. Eventually reaching her hot softness, in awe of how wet Isla had become. With her mouth she slowly sucked and licked, enjoying every single taste of her.

"Please fuck me. I need you inside of me so badly," Isla moaned louder, her legs tensing around Alex's body.

"Say please one more time, like you mean it," Alex demanded as her fingers traced up to Isla's swollen clit, lightly brushing against it.

"Please," Isla groaned, edging her body towards Alex's hand.

Before she could take her next breath, Alex pushed her fingers deep inside, curling them up slowly, entranced by the hot, wet mess in front of her. She started fucking Isla slowly, deeply, greedily. The fucking continued into a harder and faster pace. Isla found herself gushing over Alex, soaking the fabric around her thighs.

"Fuck, I think I'm going to cum already," Isla whimpered.

"You can come when I tell you," Alex replied, slowing the pace as her other hand began massaging her clit.

Isla's moans grew louder as Alex slowly fucked and massaged her into a whole new level of pleasure. Her hands and mouth kissing, touching, sucking. Tasting Isla and feeling her hot wetness. She loved to see Isla's eyes rolling back with total pleasure, as she fucked her deeper and harder. She continued to please her, enjoying every single second of it. Isla's body tensed up as goosebumps covered her beautifully soft skin. Alex replaced one of her hands with her mouth and moved her own wet fingers down to her swollen core, which was begging to be touched. She started rubbing circular motions in time with her tongue on Isla's soft folds. Her body tingling, building slowly through her core.

"You're close, aren't you? You can cum for me now. Cum hard for me, sweetheart. I want to taste it. I'm cumming for you too."

Alex pressed her mouth harder into Isla's hot

core as she came so hard and deeply for her. They both reached a new level of climax together, moaning and grabbing at each others skin. The chemistry unmatched. Their bodies tangled and tensing. Their skin puckered and hot. Alex laid over Isla, kissing her softly. She couldn't get enough of her.

"I have no words," Isla whispered.

"Me neither," Alex laughed as she rolled next to her, slowly stroking her body and realizing that she may have crossed a boundary that she couldn't undo this time.

∼

Alex woke over an hour before her alarm was scheduled to go off. It was still dark outside, and she could barely pick out the elements of her bedroom that were so familiar it was often like they weren't even there.

But Isla was here. She'd been draped over Alex for half the night, but now, she was curled up toward Alex, her hands clinging to Alex's arm as if she held all the answers and comfort the poor woman needed. Alex watched Isla for a moment, her wild hair more wild than usual as it poofed up around her face and splattered against the deep blue pillows.

Carefully, Alex reached over and brushed the curls from her face, where it almost looked like Isla was smiling.

"Suddenly this doesn't feel very casual," Alex whispered silently to herself, cautiously pulling her arm away from Isla's grip as she slid from the bed with a sigh. The panic started to set in. The familiar feeling of running a thousand miles from anyone that made her feel anything.

Alex got ready for the day as silently as possible, keeping an eye on Isla to make sure she didn't wake up before Alex was gone. Luckily for Alex, Isla slept deeply throughout the early morning. Alex left a note in the kitchen, hoping Isla would understand, but still at a loss for what this meant for their jobs.

Alex had loved every second of kissing, holding, and being with Isla last night, but somehow that made the reality of things even worse. She groaned as she slipped out the front door and began walking aimlessly away from a home that was far too different, now. She tried to tell herself it wasn't *just* because Isla was there, or because she'd spent the night, or because Alex had slept with her, but she knew she was kidding herself.

Isla was an angel. She worked hard and tirelessly to do a job well done. She cared a lot and clearly loved a lot, and Alex had taken it all for granted.

"Sarah's gonna hate me," Alex muttered to herself as she turned a corner, pausing as a stream of wind seemed to push right through her. She shivered.

"God, why'd I have to screw it all up?" Alex balled her hands up into fists, continuing toward town.

It was certainly too soon to say that she *loved* Isla, but Alex felt that she *could* love Isla—if she let herself. Not that any of her other attempts at love had really worked out.

Alex groaned again, pulling her jacket around herself and shuffling forward. She'd had sex with her best friend's younger sister of all people. Who in the world would want to be friends after something like that?

"Maybe she'd understand..." Alex mumbled to herself, pausing to wonder if...if she *really* needed to... if she could actually just drop Sarah from her life, but she immediately hated the bitter words the second they entered her mind. She knew that was a lie. Not only did she care for Sarah more than anyone and desperately wanted to continue their friendship, but Sarah had also been there for some of the darkest points of Alex's life, and this was supposed to be her stepping up to do the same. Dropping Sarah was entirely out of the question, but despite her unwillingness to entertain the thought, dropping Isla...wasn't.

In fact, the more Alex thought about it, the more she wondered if dropping Isla completely might be for the best. Clearly neither of them wanted to be just friends and trying to maintain this little charade was bound to hurt both Sarah and Isla in the end. Better to end it now before it goes too far. Better to avoid than feel. Alex had a long-standing familiarity with burying her emotion under an icy exterior. She could quite easily separate sex from emotion.

Alex found herself at a coffee shop that she and Sarah had visited a few years ago. It was stupid early in the morning, but they were open, so Alex stepped inside and bought herself a warm drink.

Perhaps Alex could speak with Trina today before Isla was scheduled to come in. She'd simply explain that both she and Isla needed to keep a better work-life balance, and she'd make sure their work lives were separate for the remainder of the time there. Trina could switch Isla's position with someone else, or maybe Isla would simply be willing to work a different shift if she were asked.

This is more difficult than I thought... Alex thought.

The woman approaching with Alex's drink in hand offered it with a gentle smile.

Alex gave a quick thank you in reply, but thankfully the employee went back to her own business without making conversation.

Alex didn't know entirely how to go about it, but she knew that keeping her and Isla separate was a must from now on. She let herself feel far too much. She just hoped Isla remembered her comments about it being casual. Alex told herself anything to pretend she wasn't about to trample all of Isla's sweet, loving heart

But it was decided. No more of Isla working in her office—and no more apologies outside public areas of the workplace. No more kissing, and no more passionate nights full of longing and...something that could have been love.

And most importantly, no more dancing.

6

ISLA HART

When Isla woke up after the most passionate night of her life, her mind flooded with images of it. The closeness of Alex she had lusted over. The feelings that flew around her heart as suddenly Alex appeared to let down her icy walls. Could this be something real? Could this be the start of Isla and Alex falling in love?

But the moment Isla turned over in bed to find it empty was the moment it all came crashing down.

Alex wasn't home. She'd left who knows how early in the morning with nothing but a note that Isla nearly missed:

I'm sorry. I can't do this with you. It went too far and I know I've made a huge mistake. Please forgive me, Isla. You deserve so much more than me. It has to be this way.

Take anything from the kitchen for breakfast.

Isla had scrunched up her face at the note, irritated that there was no indication of where Alex had gone, or why she couldn't bear to say she was sorry to Isla in person. Isla hadn't been sorry. She'd filled her head with hope and fantasy. She scoffed in anger and sighed in desperation.

How could I ever trust her, I should've seen this coming, Isla thought to herself. Amazed this was the same woman who had made her feel like a million dollars less than twenty-four hours ago.

Isla tore up the note and threw it away, grabbing her things and not bothering to take Alex up on the free breakfast. Instead, she responded to Sarah's worried texts with some fabricated story of spending the night at a friend's house as she headed home to prepare herself for the workday.

Distracting herself from her pressing torrent of emotions was going to be difficult, but she knew if she let herself have one moment to really process what had happened, she might just burst. So instead, she hurried home, doing anything she could to blast music in her ears, respond to messages from the night before, and ignore anything to do with Alex Chapman until she was somewhere she could let her emotions out.

Isla arrived at her apartment weary eyed. She lived alone, but sometimes she would spend the night with Sarah and their mom. It was only recently that Isla had moved out, and frankly, she'd often wondered if she made the right choice in doing so, but Sarah always insisted she didn't want to be in the way of Isla's independence, so she didn't push it.

Everything was just as she'd left it the morning before, and she wasted no time in hurrying to her room to get ready for the day. Her face lit up in a blush anytime she thought about Alex's kisses, or the way she'd looked at Isla with so much want. She nearly went weak in the knees just thinking about how Alex touched her. It was beyond anything she felt before and suddenly it had all disappeared. She'd never really done anything like a one-night stand, but if Alex had her way, it seemed that was all this was going to be.

Isla bit her lip as she rushed to prepare breakfast for herself.

"God, why does she make me feel like this? I'm

a fool," Isla mumbled to herself as she grabbed some toast, not even really that hungry but knowing she needed to eat. Her mind kept jumping around between their sweet night of bliss and the feeling of unease that was growing in her chest at the thought of interacting with Alex in person.

Maybe Alex wouldn't be at work? Maybe Isla could simply avoid her, at least for the day or until she had a chance to figure things out in her head.

With a glance at the door, she sighed.

Isla was in no way prepared to talk to Alex about it, at least not now.

She'd hoped that perhaps their night together meant they would be together or would at least open them up to talk about things like that, but right now, she just felt embarrassed that it had even happened in the first place. Especially because now it just felt like Alex didn't want her at all.

Isla shook her head, holding back tears as she stepped out to her car. She couldn't afford to cry over this, not until she got through work and had a moment to really think things through. She just hoped she wouldn't have to see Alex again before that happened.

Isla arrived at work just a few minutes late to find Trina waiting for her.

"Hi Trina! Sorry I'm late. Did you have a specific assignment for me this morning?"

Trina nodded, seeming a bit more distant than normal. "Yes, I'm permanently assigning you to a new area, actually."

Isla blinked in surprise. "What?"

"I think your skills would be best suited elsewhere," Trina continued. "I've assigned you to the main lobby. Some of your duties will still be the same, though. Bethany will be taking your old assignment, but she'll be with you today to walk you through the area, does that sound okay?"

Isla furrowed her brow, opening her mouth to speak and pausing for a second before finally saying, "Why am I being moved now?" Her thoughts dug deeper, coming out in words before she had a chance to think them through. "Does this have to do with Alex?"

Trina sighed, "If you're talking about Ms. Chapman, I'm afraid I can't say. But I will say that I'm sorry to move you so suddenly after you were just getting used to the position."

So it *was* Alex.

Isla cursed in her head, taking a deep breath and nodding. "It's fine. I can take the new assignment."

Trina thanked her, but the atmosphere was clearly already an uncomfortable level of awkward. Even if it wasn't that day, Isla had hoped she could talk with Alex and get this mess figured out before long, but it seemed that Alex was avoiding her.

Isla had been determined not to even see Alex that day, but after hearing that Alex had just moved her to a different area without even talking to her, she felt like something needed to be said. Even if she wanted to run away from the situation herself, Isla knew it would only make things far worse, so she wouldn't let Alex stay away for long.

With careful breaths, Isla grit her teeth and followed Trina to meet with Bethany, doing her best to stay distracted and calm as they went through each step of the workday.

Isla ignored thoughts of Alex's frantic hands as she scrubbed tables and chairs. She pushed aside reminders of their night together by spraying an exorbitant amount of cleaner on the windows. And she nearly shoved a chair across the room before thinking better of it. She felt mad, madder than she'd ever felt, but if she was being honest with herself, it was all stemming from fear.

Fear that she'd never have that again, that everything was her fault, that Alex hated her and wanted her out of her life forever. Maybe she'd even push Sarah out of her life.

Isla winced at the thought, shaking her head as she carefully pulled herself to her feet. The lobby was clean enough for now. Spotless, even. She'd have plenty of time to finish up later.

Without a second thought, Isla put down her rags and bottles and stepped purposefully to the elevator, which brought her up to Alex's floor. She marched through the halls, her heart hammering in her chest. It wasn't until she was at the door that Isla finally paused.

It took a few careful breaths for Isla to let herself knock, and even then, her touch was light and careful, with all the anger melting away into something much more sharp and anxious inside her. Alex responded quickly, as always, but maybe it was too quick. Maybe she knew it was Isla at the door.

While biting her lip in an attempt to distract herself from her bubbling emotions, Isla cracked the door open, carefully slipping inside while she watched Alex with wary eyes.

"Yes, what is it..." Alex called promptly as her head rose up, face falling at the sight of Isla.

Isla couldn't help but frown. The two of them stared in silence, then, after a moment, Isla let out a careful breath, "You...you know what..." Her thoughts stumbled into nothing as she carefully shut the door behind her.

Alex's eyes narrowed ever so slightly, her rigid features seeming more and more frightening the longer those silent seconds stretched out. "If I already know, then why are you here?"

Isla pursed her lips, nodding more to herself than to Alex. "I...I just want to know *why*."

Alex raised a brow, clearly waiting for Isla to explain further.

Isla hesitated, disturbed by how drastic the change in Alex was from the night before. "Why..." she started, biting her lip before continuing, "Why did you invite me over and sleep with me, only to pretend like it never happened? You're driving me crazy."

Isla held her breath. She didn't particularly want an answer, because what answer would be good there? Ultimately, some answer had to be better than none, and she couldn't deal with this happening a third time with no explanation.

Alex took a few moments to respond, only adding to Isla's worries, but she finally spoke in a low and careful tone that made all the confidence in Isla fizzle out. "Because for all intents and purposes of our working relationship and our relationship with your sister, it didn't."

Isla's heart dropped. She couldn't hide the disappointment from her eyes. "What?"

Alex remained steady in her gaze and demeanor. "It didn't happen. It shouldn't have happened in the first place, so I've taken measures to ensure it does not happen again. Just by being here, you're fighting against those measures. Don't you agree that it's better this way? To stop before it goes too far"

Isla's insides were twisting in on themselves. Every word from Alex just seemed to make the situation worse. It had already gone too far.

"What? No, of course not! You're being ridiculous, Alex. If you want to cut me out of your life then so be it, but you can't do so without telling me why. You just decided this all on your own!"

"And why would I owe you an explanation?"

"Because your actions last night can't go

without consequences!" Isla stuttered in growing agitation. "You-you invited me over, you made a move, and you kept pushing for more because you knew I wanted it. You weren't just messing with me, were you?"

Something in Alex's steady demeanor seemed to crack. "No, I wasn't flirting just to mess with you."

"Then why were you?" Isla demanded, feeling something prick at the back of her eyes.

Alex sighed, keeping eye contact for a moment longer before turning away and back into her cold and frosty presence. "Isla. I like you, that doesn't mean I love you or am committed to you. Clearly, you're looking too much into this. Yes, it was inappropriate of me to make a move on you, but move on already. You shouldn't be so upset about this. We had a casual fling and that's that."

Isla's breath caught in her throat. She was doing all she could to hold back the tears, but somehow, she couldn't hold back the words that she hadn't fully thought through herself as they stumbled from her lips. "It wasn't just a fling to me, Alex. I've been crushing on you for years, did you really have no idea?"

Alex turned her eyes back to Isla in a sharp

glare. "It sounds like you're just making things up now, Isla."

"What?!" Isla's heart hammered in her chest, threatening to burst. "You think I'd make that up?"

"Listen, Isla." Alex began, and Isla was surprised at herself that she stopped. "I know how desirable it can be to...be with an older woman. You're cute and sweet, but you're just too young to understand how these things work. This isn't a fairy-tale, it's the real world."

"What?" Isla furrowed her brow. "What do you mean I'm too young?" Isla asked abruptly, stepping back and clenching her fists. "I'm 34, not some... some child!"

"That's just it," Alex interjected. "You're over a decade younger than me. And as lovely as it could be to keep something going between us, we simply can't with the prior relationships we have."

Isla opened her mouth to speak, but Alex beat her to it, slowly rising from her chair in a way that made Isla want to cower under the desk.

"On top of that, it seems to me that we don't want the same things in a *relationship*." Alex drew out the last word, sighing softly, and looking at Isla as if it were a monumental task for her to understand something as simple as this.

Isla's eyebrows scrunched up, her face contorted in a mixture of confusion, anger, hurt, and betrayal. "Do you not want a relationship?"

"No." Alex shook her head. "Did I not make that clear?"

Isla shrunk back, slowly losing her ounce of confidence. "Then why make a move in the first place?" Isla pleaded, uncertain why Alex wouldn't answer her.

Alex let out a deep sigh. "You're going in circles, dear," she said sternly. "We all have wants, we all have needs, but for me, a relationship with you does not fall into either of those categories. I did reiterate to you last night that it was just casual."

Isla took a tentative step forward, determined to find out what the real answer was. "That can't be it," Isla continued. "I thought there was something between us, something more real than that. I can feel it, but you hide it so deep you trick yourself into thinking it's fake." Her lip began to wobble as she spoke. "Haven't you been in a relationship before? Or if not, have you ever wondered if you're just scared of what that might entail?"

"Scared?" Alex scoffed, muscles tensing. "Of course I'm not scared. You're grasping at straws,

Isla," Alex added, growing more serious by the second.

Isla wanted to say something to defend herself, but Alex beat her to it.

"We're working separately from now on, and that's final, Ms. Hart."

Isla struggled to find the right words, stumbling over herself as she pleaded once more. "You really won't even let me work near you? I was doing fine before you invited me over. It still hurt, but I could deal with it." Isla sucked in a breath. "Why are you pushing me away like this? Even from us just..." Isla's voice cracked. She paused, swallowed, then added, "Just being friends?"

Similarly, Alex also paused for a moment, but instead of conveying thought and consideration in her answer, the pause only made the tension in the room that much greater. "Because we can't be *just friends*, Ms. Hart, and it appears to me that we can't keep this casual either. You're simply too immature for something like that." Alex narrowed her eyes. "And I shouldn't be encouraging that in the workplace either. So, the only way I see it moving forward is by us working separately from now on."

Isla pursed her lips, debating whether she should lash out, take the blow and leave, or try to reason with Alex. Every attempt she'd made at finding out the truth was only met with a wall. She'd had many people do this to her before, most could walk over her quite easily, but she thought maybe this time would be different. Alex was someone she knew, someone she cared about, someone she'd crushed on from afar for a long, long time, maybe without fully realizing it herself. Alex was someone her sister trusted, and someone Isla thought she trusted as well.

But the more they talked, the more confused Isla was. Her heart was twisting in knots, her soul aching for the chance to pursue this, to find a resolution, or at least some semblance of closure. But it seemed that Alex wouldn't even offer that.

"I can't believe you won't even take responsibility for your own actions," Isla's voice mumbled out through her uncertain thoughts.

Alex's eyes widened, clearly offended by the comment. Before she had a chance to speak, Isla opened her mouth once more.

"I thought you were so incredible to be my sister's best friend, to offer me this job, to work with me and help me, and you even made me feel like you actually cared, but it sounds like that was all a mistake." Isla felt a stray tear slide down her cheek, voice wavering as she spoke quieter and quieter. "What am I supposed to tell Sarah? That I failed the job? That we just weren't getting along? Or that she shouldn't have trusted you with something like this in the first place?"

Isla bit her lip, the tricky words hanging in the air between them. Alex's cool demeanor was fading, and she was clearly sick with tension, irritation, and a bubbling mess of emotions that Isla didn't have the strength to figure out right now.

"Are you going to tell Sarah?" Alex asked coolly, breaking the thick silence between them.

Isla shuffled on her feet, looking away from Alex and still biting her lip to keep the tears at bay. "Like I said, what else am I supposed to tell her?"

Alex was quiet for a long moment that stretched out into an uncomfortable silence. Eventually, she spoke, much more slowly and carefully than the rest of their heated conversation. "Fine. Whatever you do now is up to you, but I think our conversation is done."

Isla sucked in a breath, pausing, and debating whether she could make this mess into something even just slightly better. But after a moment of locking onto Alex's cold, hard stare, Isla gave in. "Fine."

Alex nodded to her, but Isla didn't bother to nod back. She turned back toward the door, letting herself out and rushing down the hall before she had a chance to think about where she was going.

With the last semblance of clarity in her mind, Isla pulled out her phone and texted Trina that she was taking the rest of the day off. She could claim being sick because it was true. She felt sick to her stomach, sick to her bones, and sick all over. She didn't stop walking until she made it back to her car and didn't stop driving until she was back home.

∼

When Sarah asked what was wrong, Isla didn't tell her. She was shocked at herself for keeping something this big from her sister, but when it came down to it, she just couldn't get the words out. She wasn't ready to tell Sarah everything, especially when so much was left unsaid, and so much was left unresolved.

Isla had become pretty well-versed in keeping up a happy face, and that wasn't any different now. She smiled through the pain when Sarah stopped by her apartment, telling her sister that she had a stomach bug and had to come home from work early. When asked about Alex, Isla praised her, telling her sister about how generous Alex was in letting her go home to rest. It was better this way.

But as soon as Sarah left and Isla made it to her room, the door shut between her and the rest of the world, the mask collapsed.

Isla fell on her bed, burying her face and gripping the sheets, desperately trying to make sense of her conversation with Alex.

Everything Alex had done while Isla worked there, in such a short time, seemed to conflict. At first, they just felt like friends. Then in a brilliant moment, they were lovers. And after that moment, they were strangers once more. And then the cycle repeated itself. And Isla didn't know if she could handle it being repeated again.

Looking over their conversation, or rather, argument, in her mind, Isla was certain she'd seen a moment of authenticity behind Alex's mask of calmness, sternness, and confidence. Maybe even regret.

Even from the little Isla knew of Alex, it made sense that Alex seemed cold from afar, but up close, she was kind, considerate, and fun to be around. She'd seen that plenty of times in watching her and Sarah interact. So in those few moments where things had been sweet between herself and Alex, or where something more than just being sweet and flirty had occurred, there had to be something real about it.

It had felt real to Isla, at least.

The way she'd danced in the office with no one to see her but Alex, that had felt real. She had felt so free, and for some reason, she'd felt that Alex had seen that in her, even just for a moment.

After so many mundane jobs and tasks in her life, after struggling to get by time and time again, after dealing with bad bosses, bad coworkers, and work conditions that made her want to cry, this has been a dream. But no more.

Maybe all of those moments the two of them had shared, maybe they were fake. Maybe it was just Isla wishing those moments of bliss upon herself.

Isla shook her head into her pillow, balling her hands up into fists and wanting to scream into the puffy fabric.

Alex had to have felt something. There must've been something there, and yet, maybe Alex was right, and Isla was just immature and not used to this type of casual relationship. But maybe Alex was the one who was wrong, and she was just afraid of what being in a relationship might entail.

"And we hardly even know each other," Isla muttered to herself, flopping over in bed to lie on her back and stare blankly at the ceiling above. As the thoughts drifted away, she let herself think of nothing, wishing that the pit of anxiety in her stomach could fade for just a few minutes of peace.

"Could we have known each other more?" Isla pondered aloud, feeling herself on the edge of tears once more. "If we'd really tried?"

Inside, a part of her still hoped for that, a part of her still yearned, but what would Sarah say? Even knowing her sister as well as she did, Isla wasn't sure if Sarah would approve of something like this. Especially with the age difference, as Alex had so brutally pointed out.

It was awkward and new, strange and almost exciting, but altogether it felt like the world was telling her it was wrong. Was Alex the one person who could make Isla happy? She didn't know. But could things have been good if they'd tried, at least for a bit? Isla certainly thought so.

Isla grabbed the nearest pillow, pulling it into her and curling up on her side. She didn't want to think about this right now. She still felt sick, but

ALEX CHAPMAN

The moment that Isla left her office, all of Alex's walls dropped. Her face fell, and her heart sank, and she felt a sickness in her stomach that made her want to curl up on the floor and cry.

The sensation wasn't entirely new to her, but it had been a long, long time since she had felt that way, especially when it involved another person.

Alex knew she'd messed up. Frankly, this whole situation would be so much better if things just went back to the way they were before she gave Isla the job.

Now, she was at the risk of losing her best friend and making an enemy of her best friend's sister forever. And on top of that, she was hurting these two sisters more than they ever deserved, all while they were trying to support their sick mother. What kind of monster does that?

Alex tried to get herself back into work, even just trying to whip out a few designs like she normally would after a stressful day, but it seemed that even her own talents were upset with her.

Within a couple of hours, Alex found herself calling up Sarah and arranging to meet.

Sarah wasn't available until the evening, so each hour leading up to that, Alex grew more and more uncomfortable.

Isla was such a sweetheart, and she really didn't deserve the pain this was causing her, but having a relationship just simply wasn't an option. Alex wasn't ready to commit to something like that, and Isla surely wasn't either. Sure, she was adorable, kind-hearted, shy, and better than anyone Alex had dated before, but the fact of her being Sarah's sister still remained. Not that she'd even have a chance now after blowing everything with Isla multiple times. She'd rather dig her heels in deeper and put a stop to this rather than try to wade through this mess she'd made.

Even if the thought made her somewhat

queasy, ultimately, Alex decided that telling Sarah the truth would be better than making up more lies. Or at least, some of the truth. She'd already hurt Isla enough, and hopefully, this would be the end of it.

Once she made it to the bar, Alex was set in her decision to tell Sarah as much as she could, maybe try to fix things as best she could, and leave it at that. There was little chance she could actually fix things with Isla, but she didn't have to sacrifice Sarah in the process.

"Alex!" Sarah called out eagerly, shuffling up to the entrance of their favorite bar, only using one crutch this time.

Alex waved back, attempting to smile politely and mimic her energy, but Sarah could immediately see right through her.

"Are you doing okay?" Sarah asked in concern, pulling Alex into a quick side hug.

Alex waved the question aside. "Oh, I'm fine. It's just been a long day."

Sarah still looked concerned, but she seemed to know well enough that Alex wasn't about to open up until they'd had a couple of drinks. Instead, she nodded, linking her arm in Alex's like they did back in college, and stepped swiftly into the bar, leaning on her slightly for support.

The bar was bustling, but not too loud. Just like Alex liked it.

Sarah stayed quiet while they grabbed drinks, keeping a bright smile on her face until she was suddenly pulling Alex over to a secluded corner.

The two of them sat down at an empty table with drinks in hand, and Alex spared no time in taking a large swig of her drink.

"Whoa there, girl," Sarah said. "You don't drink like that unless someone's challenged you or you're stressed. Can you tell me what's up?"

Alex avoided Sarah's gaze, shrugging and taking another sip before setting the drink down with a loud sigh. "Too much for just one drink to fix, am I right?"

Sarah rolled her eyes, watching Alex carefully. Strangely, it made Alex nervous to see Sarah so fixated on something. Normally, she'd at least laugh with Alex about her joke before getting to the point.

"What?" Alex asked, trying to prolong the inevitable for as long as she could.

Sarah sighed, "I know you're stalling. Does this have to do with Isla?"

Alex immediately sat up straight in her seat. "W-what? Why would you say that?"

"Well, for starters," Sarah began slowly, "That was a pretty suspicious reaction for someone who didn't have something going on with my sister."

Alex grimaced, letting out a sharp breath through her teeth. "Okay, you got me. It does have to do with Isla."

Alex waited for Sarah to burst into a torrent of accusations, but she was silent, clearly eyeing Alex and waiting for her to continue.

"Ugh, fine," Alex whispered through gritted teeth, still struggling to meet Sarah's eye. "I invited you here to tell you what's been up between us. You know your sister is...my type. While we've been working together, I made some moves I shouldn't have, and...one thing sort of...led to another. Got a bit out of control, if you know what I mean."

Sarah narrowed her eyes. "What did you do to her?"

"I didn't do anything!" Alex started, then stopped herself, wincing as she spoke. "I...well, like I said, I made some moves. She's been interested in me as well, and this wasn't anything to hurt her, I promise, but things got out of hand even when I tried to end it between us. I'm sorry."

Sarah pursed her lips, taking a slow breath in and out, speaking with words that sounded like ice. "I'm gonna need more than a *sorry*. I know Isla was at your house the other night, and she's been distraught since then. What exactly did you do?"

"Fine." Alex stopped herself from saying anything more, instead, settling on the simplest answer. "I slept with her."

"You what?!" Sarah raised her voice, eyes growing wide and furious.

Alex held her hands up in defense. "What did you think was going to happen when she spent the night at my house?"

"I thought you'd at least show some restraint!"

"Listen, Sarah, I know I shouldn't have—" Alex began, unsettled by Sarah's rage.

Sarah shook her head and interrupted Alex. "Then why didn't you stop? Frankly, from what little I've heard from Isla, she's much more upset about whatever happened *after*. Did you even think of the consequences of something like that?"

"I'm sorry, I didn't. You know I'm like this, and I really tried because she's your sister."

"Just because she's my sister?" Sarah asked incredulously.

"Well, not *just* because of that," Alex began, but she knew it was a blatant lie. They both did.

Sarah scoffed. "Whether or not she's my sister shouldn't matter. Isla doesn't go about dating like you do, and if she likes you enough to want to sleep with you, then she must *really* like you. Why'd you have to give her what she wants only to hurt her?"

"I didn't mean to hurt her," Alex interjected. "Truly, it was the last thing I wanted to happen."

Sarah stood up from her seat, reaching for her crutch. She hadn't even touched her drink. "Well, you did, and you're only making it worse by talking to me instead of her."

Sarah moved to step past Alex, but Alex quickly grabbed her wrist, stumbling to her feet and looking at Sarah with what she was sure was more distress than she'd felt in a long time. "Please, wait. Just hear me out."

Sarah paused, still furious, but Alex figured she might as well take her chance now.

"Listen, I know I messed up big time. I made a huge, shitty mess of everything by trying to keep my distance and failing. I keep trying to push past this like it's just a one-night stand, but..."

Alex hesitated, biting her lip. She could feel Sarah's gaze boring into her. "But I don't know if that's what it was this time..." She couldn't meet Sarah's eye.

Through her grip on Sarah's wrist, Alex felt the tension slowly drain out of her. Upon looking up, she saw a softer, more curbed version of Sarah's anger. She pulled her hand back and sat back down without a word. Alex followed suit, feeling entirely out of place and far too vulnerable for her liking.

"I know I have issues with relationships," Alex mumbled softly. "I know I don't...commit well to these things, but I haven't stopped feeling awful from the first time I kissed your sister and pushed her away for being...well, your sister." Alex looked at Sarah pleadingly.

"Do you actually like her? Or do you just like sleeping with her?" Sarah asked softly, the iciness of her voice melted but still cold.

Alex slowly nodded, still pondering on the thought herself. "I...I think so? I'm not certain what I feel for Isla at this point, but I know it's more than just sleeping with her. I promise. She's been kind, thoughtful, and eager. She makes me laugh, and you know that doesn't always come easy for me. And she's so beautiful and... sexy."

Sarah raised a brow.

"Sorry." Alex held up a hand in defense, taking a slow breath that slowly settled into silence.

Sarah was quiet for a few more moments, but she seemed significantly more relaxed since her outburst. "Well, good," she sighed. "I still don't like it though. Like you said yourself, you don't do well with commitment. I love that girl and when she hurts I pick up the pieces." Sarah paused, then took a sip of her drink.

Alex took a slow drink herself, contemplating what it would mean if she did commit to something more with Isla. Sarah was silent, and for the first time in years, the silence felt awkward between the two of them. Eventually, Alex spoke up.

"If I'd told you before all this that I was attracted to your sister, what would you have said? Would you have been okay with it?"

Sarah swirled her drink, brows knitted in deep thought. "I...I don't know that either. I can definitely see the two of you working well together... I think the hardest part has been seeing how sad

Isla has been because of this." Sarah took a sip of her drink before continuing. "I just want you both to be happy. You've each been through a lot, and a lot of different things, but if you two had told me that this made you happy after all that…well, that's all I'd want to hear."

Alex nodded, letting out a held breath. Frankly, it was a better response than she'd expected, but she still felt sick all over. Taking another sip of her drink now felt like something that would make her explode, so she set the glass down gently. "I'm sorry I've been so immature about this, and I'm sorry I didn't talk to you sooner."

Sarah nodded, but then the silence dragged on again while the two of them sat in their thoughts.

Alex desperately hoped that Sarah might speak up and break the silence or change the subject, but it was too late for that now. Alex finished her drink without realizing it, feeling sicker than ever, but she fought through it until the pain was bearable enough to speak again.

"Where is she?" Alex asked hoarsely.

Sarah cocked an eyebrow. "Why do you want to know?"

Alex sighed. "I just want to make things right, for real this time." She paused. "I…I don't have a plan, I don't know what Isla will say, but I at least want to set my actual feelings out there before pushing her away for good. I...I want to hear her out, and really listen. I need a god damn good therapist too."

Sarah seemed to almost smile at that. "I'm happy to hear that." With a slow breath, she nodded, pulling out her phone and swiping through a few apps. "Here, I'll send you her address. Just please don't hurt her again, okay? She's been through enough, and I don't think you give her enough credit for how mature and smart she is. Sort your fucking commitment issues out too."

Alex felt her phone buzz as Sarah put hers away, and she gave her friend a thankful smile and a nod. "Thank you. I will." Slowly, Alex pulled herself to her feet. "If she says no, I guess that's that, but I'm going to go work things out, I promise."

Sarah nodded, waving her away. "Alright, then go already. Take care of her for me."

"I will." Alex nodded, making sure to pay for their drinks before heading out into the cold night air.

Isla's apartment was closer than Alex had thought. In just a few minutes, she was parked right outside the building with the sick feeling inside her melding with the pounding of her heart. It was one thing to tell Isla they couldn't be anything when she was a CEO running a company but entirely different when she felt like a young woman giddy at the thought of chasing down love.

Alex had never let herself really get close to anyone, not past a few dates that didn't mean much more than a pleasurable night out. It always made her feel scared, just like Isla had suspected. But strangely, what was scarier right now, was the prospect of missing out on a chance to have real love with no way of ever going back to it. She already felt like she'd gone too far in pushing Isla away, but Isla was so much better than her, and maybe she could see passed that to the part of Alex that did want this and was furious with herself for fighting against it.

Alex stepped out of the car with her sleek jacket bundled around her. She walked along the path by Isla's apartment building, reading through numbers until she found the one belonging to Isla.

She was on the second floor on the far right, and thankfully, her light was still on. Taking a peek at her watch, Alex noted that it was just after 10 PM, late, but not horribly so.

Without a second thought, Alex knocked on the door. She waited a few seconds, but there were no footsteps, no movements from inside, and no click from Isla unlocking the door.

Alex took the moments that stretched on and on and on and readied herself. She knew she was far from perfect when it came to actual relationships and letting people in, but the best she could do is really try, and keep working on herself in the meantime. If Isla actually wanted this, she could make time, and she *would* make time. More than anything, Alex hoped she'd be able to see Isla smile again. Maybe even dance.

After nearly a minute had passed, Alex lifted her hand to knock once more, but the door swung inward and there stood Isla, dumbstruck in a full face of makeup, hair half done up in the sweetest little braids, and a long dress with a slit down the side that Alex couldn't help but be drawn to for a split second.

"Alex!" Isla exclaimed, confusion clouding her

8

ISLA HART

Isla had finally decided to wait and worry about Alex in the morning. She'd been stressed all day about what she should do about the whole messy situation, but thankfully, a few of her friends were meeting up at a party, and although it wasn't Isla's kind of scene, it might be the perfect opportunity to get her mind off of things.

She'd picked out what she hoped was a flattering dress in a beautiful golden yellow color, and she'd taken the time to tame her hair more than she would for a normal workday. Looking at herself in the mirror, she'd say she looked pretty good, smiling at herself as she turned about.

A knock at the door startled Isla out of her preparations. She threw on the closest coat and grabbed her phone and wallet, just in case Silvia was stopping by early to pick her up. It took her longer than she expected to get to the door.

Upon opening it, she expected a beaming grin and a pink dress, but instead, she was met with a professional-looking but muted Alex, looking far too reserved and unsure than she had any right to be.

"Alex?" Isla's face scrunched up in confusion. Then, her expression turned slightly sour, despite her best efforts to remain pleasant. "Why on earth are you here?"

Alex took a deep breath, pulling herself out of a slouch. "Can we talk?"

Isla pursed her lips. "Talk? Are you going to try and charm me only to break my heart, *again*? What the hell is up with you? You are so hot and cold." The words came out much more antagonist than she'd meant, but perhaps ignoring the inevitable had made her feelings build up past the point of what she could easily cover up.

"No, no, I'm not here to make a move or to try to convince you of anything. I just want to explain myself and then...let you decide."

Isla studied Alex's face, searching her eyes and waiting for the cool and frosty CEO to come back and tell Isla she was falling right into her little trap. But, strangely enough, she found none of the frostiness there. Alex seemed pained, and almost... awkward. Which, somehow, was comforting.

After a moment longer, Isla took a deep breath and responded. "I'm... I'm open to that. Come in."

Isla was surprised at herself at how easily she opened the door for Alex, but it was hard not to be surprised when Alex was acting so unlike herself. She whispered a soft, "Thank you." when entering, taking off her shoes and coat and waiting politely for Isla to direct her.

"Do you, um, do you want anything to drink?" Isla asked, glancing back at her kitchen to see if she had anything worthy of serving a guest.

Thankfully, Alex shook her head. "Thank you, but I'm alright."

Internally, Isla let out a sigh of relief. She nodded back and came to sit next to Alex, pulling out her phone to glance over the texts from her friends. "One sec," she whispered, sending a quick text to the group to let them know to go without her. Isla was a little sad at the prospect of missing out, but if she really had an actual, genuine chance with fixing things with Alex here she wanted to take it.

"Sorry about that," Isla whispered, setting her phone aside.

"It's no problem." Alex smiled softly, her face looking somewhat foreign at the calm and sweet gesture. "Did you have plans tonight?" she added, voice on the edge of concern.

Isla waved a hand in front of her. "Oh, it's fine. I was just going to head out with some friends, but we'll go another time. This, um... This sounds important." Isla took a careful breath, slowly meeting Alex's eye and struggling not to blush. "What did you want to talk about, exactly?"

Alex nodded. "Well, I wanted to be honest with you." She took a moment more to gather her thoughts, trying to smile in a way that made her seem so much smaller and less threatening than before. "I've been pushing you away because... because I thought it was wrong of me to like you, since you're Sarah's younger sister."

Isla suspected that was the case, but she nodded along and let Alex continue.

"I didn't want to push her away, but I was indirectly pushing both of you away. I also have a fuckton of issues around commitment. I'm basically a mess. People think I'm this headstrong, ice queen bitch who has it all, but inside I have battles."

Isla noticed Alex fiddling with her fingers. It was something she'd never noticed from Alex before. She always seemed so sure of herself, and the more Alex didn't seem sure, the more Isla wasn't quite sure what to do. Luckily, Alex seemed content to carry on without any response from Isla, at least for now.

"You said it yourself, I-I just don't do well with relationships. It's daunting to commit yourself to one person. It's a risk I haven't been willing to take, but in doing so, I've been selfish. I haven't heard you out. I haven't listened to what *you* want. And I'd like to change that."

Isla nodded carefully as she played with the thought in her mind. It was certainly comforting that Alex had been thinking about this so deeply and that she wanted to really listen to Isla, but the fear of Alex turning this around all over again was still so present. She'd been playing this sort of scenario in her mind all day, wondering what she could say, if she really wanted to commit herself to a relationship. But if she was honest with herself, she really didn't think that Alex would actually come forward and just talk like this. It was strange

—but welcome—and she hoped she had longer to contemplate what appeared to be Alex's true desire underneath the layers of rejection Isla was growing so used to.

"Why aren't you saying anything?" Alex asked softly, tilting her head to catch Isla's eye.

"O-oh, sorry." Isla sat up straight. She hadn't even realized she'd been staring into her lap. "I just... It's a lot to think about. I did not see this coming."

Alex smiled hopefully. "I know. I should have been better in thinking about this earlier. I know I hurt you in pushing you away, but I don't want to do that anymore. I actually just came back from speaking with Sarah, which I should have done in the first place, but she's more okay with it than I thought." Alex chuckled to herself. "As long as it's what we both want, and as long as we're both happy."

Isla was surprised to hear that Alex had told Sarah about their situation, but in all honesty, it was a relief to have that secret lifted, and an even bigger relief to have Sarah be okay with it in some way, shape, or form. She'd certainly have to talk with Sarah in more detail later, but before she could wonder on it any longer, she spoke.

"Is it something you want?" Isla asked without thinking, feeling a tinge of red in her cheeks. "You said before you don't want a relationship, but would us being a couple be something that makes you happy?"

Alex leaned forward, nodding slowly as she spoke. "I think so. If I'm being honest, I'm still figuring that out, but if you'll have me, I'd rather figure it out with you."

The moment Alex leaned closer, Isla felt her heartbeat speed up once more. This was feeling more and more familiar to the moment at Alex's place where she had captured Isla's lips, heart, and soul, and made her feel far more cherished than she'd ever been before. But at the same time, this moment was acutely different. Alex felt genuine. Even in her uncertainty, she felt sure. She was letting her true feelings be known and willing to let herself be hurt, just as Isla did far too easily than she cared for.

Isla met Alex's eye and began to nod, then stopped herself. "Are you sure you'll work this out *with* me? I can't go through you just dropping me again, so if you want me to give you a chance, this is your last one. If you drop me without talking through things, I'm not speaking to you again. You need to earn back my trust."

Immediately, Alex nodded. "I understand. And I *do* want to work this out with you, Isla, I really do. I've sent a message to the city's best therapist. I'm going to work through my issues and become a better person. I want to make you happy. I never want to see you sad again."

"Okay." Isla let out a held breath.

Tentatively, Alex reached forward with an open palm, whispering slowly, "I know I'm new to it, but I want us to figure this out together. To mess up and make up together. I'd like to take the chance at finding real love with you, however corny that might sound."

Isla couldn't help but scoff in disbelief at Alex being so cheesy. She smiled though, carefully taking Alex's hand and squeezing it gently.

The two of them looked each other in the eye, and the moment felt somewhat final, as if they'd made a silent agreement to work this out with one another. They both smiled. Isla felt light, like a weight was being lifted from her chest, and just by looking at her, she could tell that Alex did too.

"Sorry to keep you from your night out," Alex whispered, gently squeezing Isla's hand.

Isla shrugged. "It's okay. Talking through this was good. I just can't believe you actually like me back after you seemed so against the idea."

Alex groaned, "I know, I'm sorry. I've been a real jerk to you. And everything I said about you being too young, I didn't mean it, I promise. You're lovely just as you are, and I have just as much to figure out in this as you do."

"Well, we're in this together now." Isla smiled, scooting a bit closer to Alex and noticing her eyes drift down Isla's figure with a slight blush.

"That's a *beautiful* dress, Isla," Alex smiled. "It suits you wonderfully."

Isla's cheeks grew pinker, silently chiding herself for choosing that night of all nights to wear a more revealing dress. She normally didn't wear something so low cut, or something with a slit down the side. It was a dress her friends had coaxed her to buy that she thought she'd never wear. But even if it was embarrassing, there was a small part of her that was almost excited to have Alex see her in it.

"Thank you." Isla lowered her eyes as a smile crept onto her face. She brought her free hand up to brush a strand of hair out of her face, but Alex beat her to it.

Alex's delicate but strong hand brushed Isla's hair aside, being deliberate with each careful motion. She tucked it behind Isla's ear, tracing her ear and down to her jaw in one swift motion that seemed to stretch on and on and on.

Isla glanced up, unsure how she could already be so flustered by Alex's actions. She hadn't even *done* anything, for goodness' sake.

"There you go." Alex smiled, catching Isla's eye and carefully cupping her cheek. She rubbed her thumb there, eyes locked on Isla, much calmer than usual. Somehow, despite her piercing stare seeming softer and calmer, Alex appeared more sure than ever.

Isla opened her mouth to ask something, but no words came out.

"Are you alright, Isla?" Alex whispered, tilting her head with a sliver of concern.

Isla swallowed, nodding and shifting in her seat so she could better face Alex. "I-I'm fine." Without thinking, she reached up to place her hand atop Alex's, leaning into the touch and giving Alex a warmer smile.

Alex pulled back, sighing as she fell back against the couch and pulled Isla with her so she sat curled up at her side. Isla's face was on fire, but

Alex had already moved on to start playing with her hair, humming a little and catching Isla's startled expression with laughing eyes.

Isla took her time to relax, closing her eyes and melting against Alex. This whole situation didn't feel so bad when she just closed her eyes and thought about how warm and close Alex was. Isla always thought that Alex would be frosty up close, but she was much warmer...even warmer in her personality too.

Having Alex, her boss, in her home felt strange at first, but the more she thought about it, the more Isla realized she felt safe here. Warm and safe and happy—wasn't that all she really wanted?

Alex was twirling strands of Isla's hair through her fingers, and by the time she eventually looked up, Alex was grinning smugly at her. "You're cute, you know that right? I meant everything I said to you." Then, as Isla's face blossomed into red again, Alex's face softened. "Are you feeling better?"

Isla sighed and nodded. "Yeah, thank you. Just clearing my head was nice. Just seeing the real you is what I needed."

Alex hummed and pulled Isla a touch closer. "There was one more thing I wanted to talk with you about."

Isla's heart skipped a beat, but she forced herself to nod along and ask, "What is it?" Whatever it was, she desperately hoped it wouldn't be more energy to deal with than starting this whole conversation.

"Well..." Alex let out a long and thoughtful sigh. "I just want to make things better for you at work. Speaking as both your boss and..." Alex paused, tilting her head to catch Isla's eye, "girlfriend?"

Isla blushed and nodded, scoffing slightly to mask the ounce of embarrassment at Alex actually using the word.

"As your boss and girlfriend..." Alex continued, voice growing softer in tone, "I wanted to know if you'd be interested in a more permanent role at Chapman Signature Studios." Alex let the words hang in the air for a few moments.

"Really?" Isla spoke before she could think, pulling back from Alex to look her in the eye. "An actual job or..." She paused, brow furrowing. "You don't mean a more permanent cleaning job, right? I've definitely appreciated it, but it's not what I want for the rest of my life."

Alex chuckled. "No, not unless that's what you wanted. But there's quite a bit I think you'd be good at. More than the cleaning role. You have so much potential."

Isla leaned back into Alex again. "Like what?"

Alex hummed, pulling Isla closer by her shoulder. "Like... I think you'd be wonderful as my assistant," she teased.

Isla rolled her eyes.

"I could certainly teach you a thing or two about running a business. Or... I feel like you'd do well with the marketing team." Alex's eyes traveled over Isla in contemplation. "But seeing you in something like this makes me think you'd do best in the design aspect itself..."

Isla sucked in a breath as Alex walked her fingers up the strap of her dress.

Alex hummed again, fiddling with the strap between her fingers. "Or perhaps, you might do well as a model—my *personal* model." Alex grinned slyly. "I've been thinking of bringing back fashion design to Chapman Signature Studios. And plus, I've already seen what you have to offer as a model, so I *know* you'd be more than perfect for the position."

Isla rubbed at her reddening cheeks, unsure of exactly what to say.

Alex chuckled softly. "Sorry, a bit much?"

Carefully meeting her eyes, Isla shrugged, then shook her head. "N-no, not really. It's surprising, but not necessarily...bad."

Alex's eyes lit up with renewed excitement. "Oh? Well, that's certainly something to keep in mind then."

Alex slid her hand up the side of Isla's neck, leaning in a touch before pausing. "Although, if working together like that isn't as magical as it sounds, I would do anything and everything in my power to find you a position that suits you best."

Isla nodded, letting out a held breath. "Thank you. That's really good to hear actually."

"I'm glad." Alex leaned closer again, only inches away from Isla now. "We can figure out the details later, though; give you some time to think on it."

"Y-yeah, I'd like that," Isla stumbled out, finding herself leaning forward as well.

Alex was cupping her cheek now, her breath falling softly on Isla's lips. But instead of moving forward, she paused, held frozen in a moment of time until her words broke the silence. "May I?"

A spark of excitement shot through Isla's body. Her heart was beating quicker, her memories of their kisses and intimate moments rushing back tenfold as she imagined what the future could hold for them.

"*Please*," she whispered, moving forward before she had the chance to stop herself.

Alex met her in the kiss, and their lips joined together exactly as they'd remembered to from not so long ago. At first, they kissed soft and sweet and slow, Alex wrapping Isla up in her arms and coaxing her closer and closer and closer.

Isla was happy to oblige, humming gratefully as she clung to Alex's shirt and leaned in close, letting herself be taken by Alex's strong arms, caring hands, and passionate heart.

It wasn't long until one of Alex's hands was sliding slowly up her thigh, right up the slit on the side of Isla's dress. She teased her fingers under the fabric, causing Isla to arch toward her, gripping tighter to Alex's shirt.

Isla was sure that Alex was simply tormenting her at this rate, with a hand on her thigh and their lips locked in another beautiful dance. But then Alex tilted her head and deepened their kiss, moaning as she gripped Isla's thigh and pulled her closer.

Happy to follow Alex's lead, Isla pulled herself

into Alex's lap, carefully keeping up with Alex's increasingly eager kisses.

"This okay?" Alex whispered between kisses and heavy breaths.

Isla nodded, pulling Alex back in for more.

They quickly fell back into their old routine, pushing and pulling at each other's lips, exploring one another's mouths with their tongues, and seeking every inch their hands could cover.

Before long, Isla was on her back on the couch, and Alex was above her, lips locked on Isla's neck. Isla moaned loudly as Alex sucked at the skin, panting heavily, but refusing to stop just yet.

The straps of Isla's dress were already hanging off to the side, and she couldn't tell what would be going next, but she didn't care, as long as Alex was there with her.

Alex continued checking with Isla, making sure this wasn't going too far, but every time, Isla begged her to keep going, feeling herself grow more excited, happier, and more full of a sense of wanting this to last forever.

She was caught up in the thrill of it all, the excitement, the want, and the yearning. But beyond that, things feel different between them.

They felt complete. They felt whole. Alex wanted to make up everything to her.

And in Isla giving herself over to Alex, Isla felt that she was bridging a gap between them. She wanted this to last, not just this moment, but this connection that had blossomed between them and created something so perfect and grand.

Her hands were practically glued to Alex by this point, holding onto her bare shoulders, before sliding her hands into Alex's short, silky-smooth hair. It was softer than she'd imagined, and she wished she could play with it all the time. It wasn't until that moment, that Isla realized, as Alex's newly named girlfriend, she could.

Alex's kisses were trailing down to her collarbone. Her hand curled its way under Isla's back, pulling her close. Isla wanted Alex to kiss every inch of her, and at the rate they were going, she didn't doubt that it was a possibility.

Alex nipped at Isla's skin, causing her to whine and bite her lip. Her hands gripped at Alex's hair, and Alex practically growled in reply, a hand sliding onto Isla's hip as her heartbeat quickened.

"P-please." Isla whispered, moaning loudly as Alex kissed her again and again and again.

Alex hummed in a questioning way, her tongue

snaking out to pass over the spot she'd kissed, causing Isla to shiver in want.

"Please take me," Isla gasped, taking a few heaving breaths.

"You're all mine now," Alex whispered.

Alex slowly removed all of Isla's clothes and continued to trace her lips and fingers over her soft delicate skin. They slowly moved down onto the pile of clothes on the floor, Isla's naked body laid underneath the weight of Alex's strength. Kissing harder as the passion filled the room.

"I'm so wet for you, Alex."

Isla moaned as she parted her legs, edging herself towards Alex's hand. Without hesitation, Alex ran her fingers up Isla's thighs and slid them into the wetness in between. "Wow, you really are. So am I," Alex replied.

"Please can I touch you?"

"Well, as you asked so politely." Alex laid next to Isla on the floor and unbuckled her belt. "You can feel me now," she murmured.

Isla's hand slipped into Alex's body, amazed by the silky wetness that she encountered.

"Now take out your fingers and taste it," Alex ordered.

Giving Isla commands turned them both on more than anything.

Isla did as she was told. Slowly licking and kissing her own fingers.

"You are so beautiful. I think I've cracked it. I think I know why I'm always drawn back to you."

Isla smiled, surprised by the conversation as she laid naked on the messy, clothes-filled floor.

"Oh yeah? How come?"

"Because I think I've fallen for you," Alex whispered, as she ran her hands down Isla's waist.

Isla's jaw dropped, before she began to smile and gently laugh. "Wow, where is the real Alex and what have you done with her? Do you really mean that?"

"I do, Isla. I think I love you. I do love you. I know it."

"It might not come as so much of a surprise but, I love you too," Isla replied as her heart burst with intense emotion.

Their lips met as they laid tangled in each other's body. Alex panted as her fingers raced towards Isla's hot core, her legs parting eagerly as Alex pushed them inside of her. Kissing her deeply with every thrust. She fucked Isla slowly as her body tightened around her, pushing in another finger to stretch her open more. Alex positioned herself on top of Isla, kneeling in between her legs. Continuing to fuck her and picking up the pace. Every thrust made Isla moan louder with pleasure. Curling her fingers inside of her, hitting all the right places. Alex's other hand massaged Isla's swollen clit. Slowly circling around it as she fucked her deeper.

"You're tightening already. Are you close?"

"So...fucking...close," Isla moaned as her body tensed and she reached climax just from Alex's words. She turned her on so fucking much. Alex moaned as Isla did, enjoying watching her body tense and jerk from the pleasure she could give to her. She watched Isla cum and started to remove her pants before laying next to her.

"I can't get enough of you, Alex," Isla murmured as she reveled in the post orgasmic haze.

"I want you to taste me."

Isla bit her lip as she kissed Alex.

"No, not there," Alex said as grabbed Isla's hand and moved in between her thighs. "I want you down there. It won't take long," Alex ordered.

Without anymore words, Isla moved down Alex's body and teased around her soft folds before lapping at her wetness. Her tongue moved slowly up and down, in and out, tasting and loving every part of it. Alex ran her fingers through Isla's hair at the top, slowly stroking her. "Good girl," she whispered as her hips thrust into Isla's face.

Isla's tongue darted inside of her, before her lips pursed and sucked, kissed, nibbled and devoured everything she could of Alex.

"Don't stop that," Alex murmured.

Isla continued to please her as she felt her thighs tense. Her body reached climax as she came into Isla's mouth. Alex's body thrusting between Isla's soft mouth and the hard floor.

"Fuck," Alex groaned as she reached the peak of it all. Her body relaxing after the wave of pleasure filled her mind and body. They exhaled together with happiness as Isla moved up into Alex's strong arms.

Laying on the floor and kissing, tangled together, filling the room with the smell of sex.

"You are perfect, Isla. I promise I will never ever hurt you again. You're mine now and I will protect you, care for you, love you. Always."

Isla smiled and blushed.

"And I will always be there for you. You always

EPILOGUE

Two years later

"I can't believe you got Isla to dance again," Sarah whispered as she and Alex watched the end of Isla's class.

Alex scoffed, "I didn't do anything, this was all her."

Sarah grinned and playfully punched Alex in the shoulder. "Come on! She's been so happy since you two finally figured everything out."

Alex grinned, "Aww, did our sickly-sweet romance finally melt your heart?"

"If anything was going to melt my heart, it wasn't going to be *that*," Sarah mumbled with a teasing grin. "I'm not gonna lie, though, it's still a bit weird to have my best friend and sister dating. Fortunately, I do think you're both better people for it."

"Um, thanks," Alex said, leaning against the wall as she idly watched Isla at work. "You really think I'm better for selling my company though?"

"Well, if you put it like that," Sarah rolled her eyes, turning her attention back to the dance class playing out in front of them. "But, yeah, I think it was a good run while it lasted. Now you have better things in store and the freedom to do even more. It's your time to finally live more and enjoy life, without constantly working."

Alex smiled, nodding along and pondering on what that freedom meant for both her and Isla. To start with, Isla had taken charge of a group of five eager young dancers. Alex and Sarah hadn't stopped talking about how cute they were since Isla took on this new class. They were always looking up to Isla with eyes of wonder and excitement, bouncing on their toes as Isla demonstrated their next routine or eagerly awaiting their turn to have Isla guide their hands and movements as they tried to dance for themselves.

Since Alex and Isla had made up, Isla had worked quite a number of odd jobs. She worked as Alex's assistant for a few months and found that she did perform quite well in the position. Maybe a little too well, as Sarah might say. Isla was a natural at keeping things organized, offering her input on designs, and supporting Alex with her hefty workload. She even learned quite a bit about running a business that had led her to put some serious consideration into starting her own. But especially after Sarah caught the two lovebirds making out in Alex's office, they all agreed that maybe it was time for a change of scenery, even if both Alex and Isla missed all the private times they had had together in those few short months.

Isla joined the design team after that, where she learned even more and found even more joy in her work. She hadn't done a significant amount of artwork growing up, but she'd dabbled here and there, and Isla really enjoyed working collaboratively with other artists, even if her passion for art was typically expressed through dance. The time she spent there was pleasant and insightful, but eventually it came to an end.

After several months, Isla felt she'd done all she could with the design team, so she decided it was time to move on to something new. It was a strange and bittersweet day when Isla left Chapman Signature Studios, and the year she spent there felt like so much longer than that, but she was grateful for every day of it, even the ones in the rocky beginning. She wondered if she would've ever fallen for Alex if she didn't step foot in that big, glorious building. She wondered if maybe they'd bump into each other with Sarah still being her best friend. She wondered if Alex would've ever looked at her that way if she wasn't so close and so intimate.

As for Sarah, she'd been applying for jobs for quite some time since she recovered from her workplace injury, but once she finally got into a good position, both she and Isla were doing better than ever.

Their mom, Aileen, was still sick, but slowly starting to recover. The three of them had family meals more often, and over time, Alex joined more and more too.

When Isla left Chapman Signature Studios, she found a position as a children's dance instructor. She taught anything from ballet to tap to jazz and more. Alex and Sarah could clearly see how much she loved it from the very beginning, and they were the ones to convince her to stay for so long.

A year later, and Isla still loved it, giggling and singing with her class, showing them how to twist and twirl and turn with ease. She would amaze them with powerful leaps, lifting her students up in the air to make leaps and bounds of their own. It was her dream job, and she could have been content to stay for many years to come, but Alex was always pushing her to seek for more, not settling for good when she could achieve something great.

Because of that, as well as Isla's personal drive to fulfill her dreams, the whole time she'd been working as a dance instructor, Isla was saving up for her own dance studio.

Time and time again, Alex had offered to pay for a studio and get Isla started, but this was the one thing Isla refused to settle on. She wanted to make her dream happen herself, and although Alex may have pulled some strings in finding Isla the perfect property for her studio, Isla was able to pay for it in full in the end, much to her excitement.

The studio was now fully constructed and just a few minutes from their home. These days, Isla would often go to the studio to decorate and finish up all those final adjustments after work. Alex went with her whenever she could, happy to offer a hand or an eye for design. In fact, she was even the one to design the logo for the studio: *Hart, Hopes, and Dreams*. In just a few weeks time, Isla and Alex would start advertising for the studio and have it up and running. With their combined expertise, both women were sure the opening would be a great success.

From across the room, Isla waved to her girlfriend and sister with a beaming grin, giving her students little treats as they ran off to be with their parents and loved ones.

Isla rushed over in a matter of seconds, pulling both girls into a hug. "I didn't know you were coming to watch today! I would have tried a bit harder if I knew you both were here."

Sarah scoffed, "You did great, Isla. You always do. You know they're gonna miss you here, right?"

Isla sighed with a slight nod. "Yeah, I'll miss them too, but I'll still be working part time while I get the new studio set up, so it's not goodbye quite yet."

"And thank goodness for that," Alex chimed in. "Not only will I be comforting you when that time comes, but I'll be comforting poor Reanna as well. You're gonna take all of her clients!" Alex added with a slight tease.

"Aww, come on, you know that's not why I'm starting my own studio," Isla whispered shyly.

"Of course not, but you know it's bound to happen. You're incredible."

Isla pulled back and let out a heaving sigh, but there was joy in her eyes. "Whatever happens, happens. I'm just thrilled it's finally here! Just let me go get changed real quick, I'll be back!"

Isla bounced off to the studio's backrooms before either woman had a chance to reply, leaving them to join in the quiet chatter of dancers, parents, and friends around them.

"You know, I don't know what you see in her," Sarah stated out of the blue.

"Hey! How can you say that?!" Alex said. "She's perfect, and you of all people should know that."

Sarah smirked back at Alex. "Oh, I know. I'm just testing you. Gotta keep you on your toes."

Alex rolled her eyes, but she couldn't help it when the question brought to mind the many reasons Isla made her smile. She was sweet; she was beautiful. She was talented, strong, and kept finding new ways to make Alex laugh. She was always so kind and considerate, always dropping anything and everything at the chance to help someone out. Or even just at the chance to spend some time with Alex.

Alex had sold off Chapman Signature Studios about six months ago, and it was in part due to how busy it made her. Some days, she felt productive, strong, and independent, and others, she realized how little time she made for her girlfriend. It was something she'd committed to back when they first got together, so by the time Isla was discussing opening up her own studio, Alex thought it was time to reevaluate how she spent her own time.

At first, Alex had started working less hours. She finally used up some long-awaited vacation time and took Isla to Hawaii, which was a much-needed break for the both of them. After that, she started taking Friday's off when she could, spending them with Isla at restaurants and bars and clubs. Heck, she even took Isla to a couple balls and galas where she absolutely wiped the floor with everyone there. That was one thing she wanted to do more of; she knew how happy it made her.

Alex beamed just thinking about it. After leaving behind her company, she'd had more time than she knew what to do with, but the one thing she knew was that she was spending it with Isla, who was more than happy to have the extra time, attention, and company.

It wasn't long before Alex began taking up some freelance work doing fashion and clothing design again. Just as she'd teased about so many years before, Isla became her personal model, and oh, how it motivated Alex to pursue a long-forgotten dream like nothing else.

Alex had also taken some time to try and reconcile things with her mother, after quite a bit of encouragement from Isla. She hadn't actually seen her mother in person for years, but Isla came with her to make the trip and talk through some things that had remained unsaid for far too many years. Ultimately, her mother still wasn't a fan of Alex's business, and even less a fan of her selling it away to pursue a casual fashion design career, but Alex managed to convince her to stop bringing it up, and for now, she was keeping to that.

With the money Alex received after selling the

company, she'd bought a nice house for herself and Isla. At first, Isla refused when seeing how expensive it would be, worrying that it was too much or that they wouldn't be able to maintain it, but after spending a few nights on their own to break the place in, Isla wasn't complaining.

Alex tried to help out Sarah too, but she was much more stubborn than her sister. For a while, she merely got by, but now she was thriving, still living with her and Isla's mother and starting to date a cute guy of her own. Alex was happy for her, and since dating Isla, she'd been able to spend more time with Sarah as well.

"How are you guys doing?" Sarah asked, leaning into Alex's line of sight.

Alex smiled. "We're great. I've had a lot more time for her lately, and I think Isla appreciates it."

"Yeah, and now she's the one that's about to be busy all the time," Sarah sighed.

"I don't mind it." Alex shrugged. "Plus, you know how much I love to watch her dance." Alex raised a brow at her friend.

"Oh, gross!" Sarah complained.

"She's a good dancer! I think I should talk about her talents more!" Alex grinned back.

"God, she's made you so insufferable."

"Maybe so," Alex laughed, "but I'm happy to be a little insufferable thanks to my darling Isla."

Sarah quieted down at that, watching the last of Isla's class depart. After a minute of silence, she carefully spoke. "I'm glad to hear you're doing well, but what do you think that looks like for you both in the long run?"

Alex looked at Sarah quizzically. "What do you mean? I'm not going to be dumping her anytime soon if that's what you're wondering."

"Oh, you'd better not!" Sarah quipped, then sighed. "But no, that's not what I meant. Not exactly. You guys have moved in together, you're doing so much to support Isla's new business, but... Is that it?"

Alex was quiet for a moment, then she started nodding. "No, that's not it. It's just the beginning, I think." She paused for a moment, then smiled warmly. "If you're asking about us getting married, I have thought about that."

"Oh?" Sarah perked up. "Really? I didn't think you'd actually consider settling down for good for like, years and years."

Alex shrugged. "I guess Isla has changed me more than you thought." She smirked. "But in all honesty, proposing to Isla has been on my mind for a while. I don't think now is the right time, but once she's got her studio figured out, I'll ask her."

"Really?!" Sarah asked, covering her mouth to mask the excitement. "But then, how would I be the maid of honor for *both* of you?"

Alex laughed. "That's what you're worried about?"

Before they had a chance to talk more, Isla was back with a beaming smile on her face. "Thanks for waiting! Were you guys busy? Or do you think we could go get dinner?"

"Dinner would be great!" Alex smiled, taking hold of Isla's hand and giving it a quick squeeze.

Sarah sighed, "I'd love to join, but I'm afraid my shift starts soon. I'll catch you both later, okay?"

Sarah caught Alex with a quick and knowing look before hugging her sister goodbye, but she was heading out before the moment had a chance to linger any longer.

"Where to?" Isla asked, clinging to Alex's arm as they stepped outside.

"Wherever you want." Alex grinned, pulling Isla close to her side. "Hmm... How about that new sushi place you mentioned the other day?"

"Oh! That'd be great!" Isla laughed, happily

walking beside Alex in the early hours of the sun setting on the horizon.

Alex leaned in and gave Isla a quick kiss, marveling at how lucky she was to have her. Somehow, all the success in the world couldn't compare to the bliss that came from having Isla by her side.

"Did you get any new clients this week?" Isla asked softly. "I know last week was slower for you."

Alex smiled. "I did get one today, but I'm okay with it being slow. I need to slow down more anyway."

"Pssh, that's not true. You thrive off of being busy all the time."

"And I'm plenty busy with you, aren't I?"

Isla blushed. "Come on…"

"Plus, I want to be available to help you get the studio up and running," Alex added with a growing sense of endearment in her eyes and voice.

"Aww, really?" Isla bounced on her feet.

"Of course, darling." Alex gave her another kiss. "You're going to be swarmed with millions of little dancers, after all."

Isla giggled, clinging a little tighter to Alex's arm. "God, I hope it's not millions. I don't think anyone could handle that."

Alex laughed along with Isla. "Well, if anyone could, it'd be you."

Isla rolled her eyes; those same dazzling eyes that sparkled in the sunset.

"But lucky for you," Alex smiled, her happy heart beaming through her own eyes, "you only have to deal with me."

Isla grinned up at her.

"At least for tonight," Alex added with a laugh.

Isla leaned into Alex with a contented sigh, smiling back happier than ever. "And that's all I need. That's perfect for me."

THANK YOU FOR READING!

Dear reader, I really hope you enjoyed Alex and Isla's story.

Thank you for reading my book.

If you could spare a few minutes to leave a review, that would be immensely appreciated too!

This book is a standalone romance in my Boss series. To check out the first book in the series head to here https://mybook.to/FFTB1

I have an exciting new series starting soon, which is extra spicy, sapphic and based around the lives of a group of friends.

To stay tuned, don't forget to check out my socials and find out when the next series starts. I'd love to hear from you.

X: @graceparkesfic

Tiktok: @graceparkesauthor

Insta: @graceparkesauthor

Facebook: Grace Parkes Author

Join my mailing list too for the latest book info, I promise I don't spam!! https://mailchi.mp/2a09276da35f/graceparkeswrites

Printed in Dunstable, United Kingdom